THE MOON OF GOMRATH

The Moon of Gomrath is a 'weird and marvellously evocative tale of Celtic mysteries, elves, spirits and strange presences felt, mingled to make high adventure for Colin and Susan – and peril for Susan. It is a timeless story, full of wonder and magic, terror and beauty. A fine author indeed, and perhaps one of a new generation of classics.'   *Books and Bookmen*

'This is a rich, generous book, studded with magical names and the bright sweep of an ancient imagery ... this whole volume is a spell.'   *Spectator*

'*The Moon of Gomrath* is not only powerful but remarkably sophisticated ... The book is full of wild and whirling adventure ... What is undeniable is that the reader is drawn right into the midst of it all.'

John Rowe Townsend, Guardian

OTHER TITLES IN LIONS

and many more

COLLINS : LIONS

Made and Printed in Great Britain by
Richard Clay (The Chaucer Press) Ltd, Bungay, Suffolk

FOR ELLEN,
ADAM AND KATHARINE

Contents

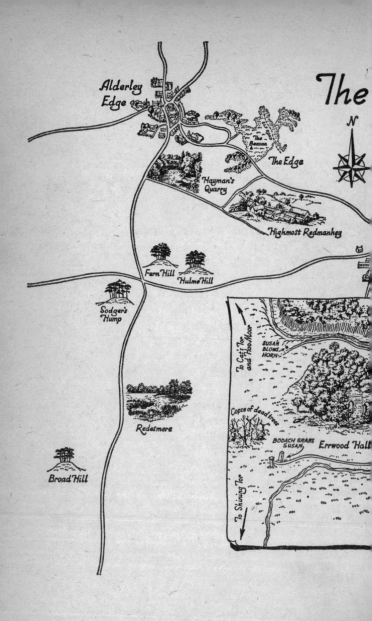

Alderley Edge

The

N

The Beacon

The Edge

Hayman's Quarry

Highmost Redmanhey

Fern Hill

Hulme Hill

Sodger's Hump

To Cat's Tor and Thoo Moor

SUSAN BLOWS HORN

Copse of dead trees

Redesmere

BODACH GRABS SUSAN

Errwood Hall

To Shining Tor

Broad Hill

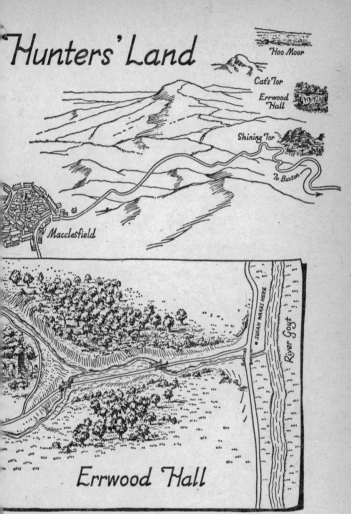

Hunters' Land

Hoo Moor

Cat's Tor

Errwood Hall

Shining Tor

To Buxton

Macclesfield

· SUSAN WAKES HERE

River Goyt

Errwood Hall

CHARLES GREEN.

'And for to passe the tyme thys book shal be plesaunte to rede in, but for to gyve fayth and byleve that al is trewe that is conteyned herein, ye be at your lyberté.'

William Caxton
31 July 1485

CHAPTER I

The Elves of Sinadon

It was bleak on Mottram road under the Edge, the wooded hill of Alderley. Trees roared high in the darkness. If any people had cause to be out in the night, they kept their heads deep in their collars, and their faces screwed blindly against the Pennine wind. And it was as well they did, for among the trees something was happening that was not meant for human eyes.

From a rib of the Edge a shaft of blue light cut the darkness. It came from a narrow opening in a high, tooth-shaped rock, and within the opening was a pair of iron gates thrown wide, and beyond them a tunnel. Shadows moved on the trees as a strange procession entered through the gates and down into the hill.

They were a small people, not more than four feet high, deep-chested, with narrow waists, and long, slender arms and legs. They wore short tunics, belted and sleeveless, and their feet were bare. Some had cloaks of white eagle feathers, though these were marks of rank rather than a protection. They carried deeply curved bows, and from their belts hung on one side quivers of white arrows, and on the other broad stabbing swords. Each rode a small white horse, and some sat proudly erect, though most drooped over the pommels of their saddles, and a few lay irrevocably still across their horses' necks, and the reins were held by others. All together they numbered close on five hundred.

Beside the iron gates stood an old man. He was very tall, and thin as a young birch tree. His white robes, and long white hair and beard flew with the gale, and he held a white staff in his hand.

Slowly the horsemen filed through the gates into the glimmering tunnel, and when they were all inside, the old man turned, and followed them. The iron gates swung shut behind him, and there was just a bare rock in the wind.

In this way the elves of Sinadon came unnoticed to Fundindelve, last stronghold of thte High Magic in our days, and were met by Cadellin Silverbrow, a great wizard, and guardian of the secret places of the Edge.

CHAPTER 2

The Well

'Eh up,' said Gowther Mossack, 'what's this?'

'What's what?' said Colin.

'This here in the *Advertiser*.'

Colin and Susan leant forward to look where Gowther's finger pointed to a headline near the middle of the page.

PLUMBING THE DEPTHS

Speculation has been aroused by the discovery of what appears to be a thirty-foot well, during excavations in front of the Trafford Arms Hotel, Alderley Edge.

While workmen employed by Isaac Massey and Sons were digging to trace a surface water drain they moved a stone flag and discovered a cavity. The lowering of a weighted string showed that the depth was thirty feet, with fifteen feet of water. The well was in no way connected with the drain, and although the whole of the covering was not removed it was estimated that the cavity was about six feet square with stone walls covered with slabs of stone.

It has been suggested that at one time there was a pump in front of the hotel and that excavations have revealed the well from which water was pumped.

Another theory is that it may probably be an air shaft connected with the ancient mines, which extend for a considerable distance in the direction of the village.

'The funny thing is,' said Gowther when the children had finished reading, 'as long as I con remember it's always been said theer's a tunnel from the copper mines comes out in the cellars of the Trafford. And now theer's this. I wonder what the answer is.'

'I dunner see as it matters,' said Bess Mossock. 'Yon's nobbut a wet hole, choose how you look at it. And it can stay theer, for me.'

Gowther laughed. 'Nay, lass, wheer's your curiosity?'

'When you're my age,' said Bess, 'and getting as fat as Pig Ellen, theer's other things to bother your head with, besides holes with water in them.

'Now come on, let's be having you. I've my shopping to do, and you've not finished yet, either.'

'Could we have a look at the hole before we start?' said Susan.

'That's what I was going to suggest,' said Gowther. 'It's only round the corner. It wunner take but a couple of minutes.'

'Well, I'll leave you to it,' said Bess. 'I hope you enjoy yourselves. But dunner take all day, will you?'

They went out from the chip shop into the village street. Among all the parked cars, the Mossocks' green cart, with their white horse, Prince, between the shafts, stood thirty years behind its surroundings. And the Mossocks were the same. Bess, in her full coat, and round, brimmed hat held with a pin, and Gowther, in his waist-coat and breeches – they had seen no reason to change the way of life that suited them. Once a week they rode down from Highmost Redmanhey, their farm on the southern slope of the Edge, to deliver eggs, poultry, and vegetables to customers in Alderley village. When Colin and Susan had first come to stay at Highmost Redmanhey everything had seemed very strange, but they had quickly settled into the Mossocks' pattern.

Gowther and the children walked at Prince's head for the short distance up the street to the De Trafford Arms, a public-house built to Victorian ideas of beauty in half-timbered gothic.

A trench about three feet deep had been dug along the front of the building, close against the wall. Gowther mounted the pile of earth and clay that stood beside it, and looked down into the trench.

'Ay, this is it.'

Colin and Susan stepped up to join him.

The corner of a stone slab was sticking out of the trench wall a little way above the floor. A piece of the slab had broken off, making a hole three inches wide : that was all. Susan took a pebble, and dropped it through the gap. A second later there was a resonant 'plunk' as it hit water.

'It dunner tell you much, does it?' said Gowther. 'Con you see owt?'

Susan had jumped into the trench, and was squinting through the hole.

'It's – a round – shaft. There seems to be something like a pipe sticking into it. I can't see any more.'

'Happen it's nobbut a well,' said Gowther. 'Pity : I've always liked to think theer's summat in the owd tale.'

They went back to the cart, and when Bess had done her shopping they continued on their round of deliveries. It was late afternoon before all was finished.

'I suppose you'll be wanting to walk home through the wood again,' said Gowther.

'Yes, please,' said Colin.

'Ay, well, I think you'd do best to leave it alone, my-self,' said Gowther. 'But if you're set on going, you mun go – though I doubt you'll find much. And think on you come straight home; it'll be dark in an hour, and them woods are treacherous at neet. You could be down a mine hole as soon as wink.'

Colin and Susan walked along the foot of the Edge.

Every week they did this, while Bess and Gowther rode home in the cart, and any free time they had was also spent wandering on this hill, searching —

For a quarter of a mile, safe suburban gardens bounded the road, then fields began to show, and soon they were clear of the village. On their right the vertical north face of the Edge rose over them straight from the footpath, beeches poised above the road, and the crest harsh with pine and rock.

They left the road, and for a long time they climbed in silence, deep into the wood. Then Susan spoke:

'But what *do* you think's the matter? Why can't we find Cadellin now?'

'Oh, don't start that again,' said Colin. 'We never did know how to open the iron gates, or the Holywell entrance, so we're not likely to be able to find him.'

'Yes, but why shouldn't he want to see us? I could understand it before, when he knew it wasn't safe to come here, but not now. What is there to be scared of now that the Morrigan's out of the way?'

'That's it,' said Colin. 'Is she?'

'But she must be,' said Susan. 'Gowther says her house is empty, and it's the talk of the village.'

'But whether she's alive or not, she still wouldn't be at the house,' said Colin. 'I've been thinking about it: the only other time Cadellin did this to us was when he thought she was around. He's either got tired of us, or there's trouble. Why else would it always be like this?'

They had reached the Holywell. It lay at the foot of a cliff in one of the many valleys of the Edge. It was a shallow, oblong, stone trough, into which water dripped from the rock. Beside it was a smaller, fan-shaped basin, and above it a crack in the rock face, and that, the children knew, was the second gate of Fundindelve. But now, as for weeks past, their calling was not answered.

How Colin and Susan were first drawn into the world

of Magic that lies as near and unknown to us as the back of a shadow is not part of this story. But having once experienced the friendship of Cadellin Silverbrow, they were deeply hurt now that he seemed to have abandoned them without reason or warning. Almost they wished that they had never discovered enchantment: they found it unbearable that the woods for them should be empty of anything but loveliness, that the boulder that hid the iron gates should remain a boulder, that the cliff above the Holywell should be just a cliff.

'Come on,' said Colin. 'Staring won't open it. And if we don't hurry, we shan't be home before dark, and you know how Bess likes to fuss.'

They climbed out of the valley on to the top of the Edge. It was dusk: branches stood against the sky, and twilight ran in the grass, and gathered black in the chasms and tunnel eyes of the old mines which scarred the woodland with their spoil of sand and rock. There was the sound of wind, though the trees did not move.

'But Cadellin would have told us if we couldn't —'

'Wait a minute!' said Colin. 'What's that down there? Can you see?'

They were walking along the side of a quarry. It had not been worked for many years, and its floor was covered with grass, so that only its bare walls made it different from the other valleys of the Edge. But their sheerness gave the place a primitive atmosphere, a seclusion that was both brooding and peaceful. Here night was gathering very quickly.

'Where?' said Susan.

'At the other end of the quarry: a bit to the left of that tree.'

'No —'

'There it goes! Sue! *What is it?*'

The hollows of the valley were in darkness, and a patch of the darkness was moving, blacker than the rest.

It flowed across the grass, shapeless, flat, changing in size, and up the cliff face. Somewhere near the middle, if there was a middle, were two red points of light. It slipped over the edge of the quarry, and was absorbed into the bracken.

'Did you see it?' said Colin.

'Yes: if there was anything there. It may just have – been the light.'

'Do you think it was?'

'No.'

CHAPTER 3

Atlendor

They hurried now. Whether the change was in themselves or in the wood, Colin and Susan felt it. The Edge had suddenly become, not quite malevolent, but alien, unsafe. And they longed to be clear of the trees: for either the light, or nerves, or both, seemed to be playing still further tricks on them. They kept imagining that there was white movement among the tree tops – nothing clear, but suggested, and elusive.

'Do you think there was anything in the quarry?' said Susan.

'I don't know. And, anyway, *what*? I think it must have been the light – don't you?'

But before Susan could answer, there was a hissing in the air, and the children leapt aside as sand spurted between them at their feet: then they saw that there was an arrow, small and white, imbedded in the path, and as they stared, an impassive voice spoke out of the dusk above their heads.

'Move not a sinew of your sinews, nor a vein of your veins, nor a hair of your heads, or I shall send down of slender oaken darts enough to sew you to the earth.'

Instinctively Colin and Susan looked up. Before them a very old silver birch threw its trunk in an arch across the path, and among the branches stood a slight figure, man-like, yet not four feet high. He wore a white tunic, and his skin was wind-brown. The locks of his hair lay close to his head like tongues of silver fire: and his eyes – were the eyes of a goat. They held a light that was mirrored from nothing in the wood, and in his hand was a deeply-curved bow.

At first, Colin and Susan stood, unable to speak, then the tension of the last few minutes broke in Colin.

'What do you think you're doing?' he shouted. 'You nearly hit us with that thing!'

'Oh, the Donas! Oh, the holy Mothan! It is himself that can speak to elves!'

Colin and Susan started at the sound of this rich voice that welled with laughter. They turned, and saw another small, but stockier, figure standing on the path behind them, his red hair glowing darkly in the last light. They had rarely seen such an ugly face. It was big-lipped, gap-toothed, warted, potato-nosed, shaggily thatched and bearded, the skin tanned like brambles at New Year. The left eye was covered with a black patch, but the right eye had the life of two in it. He was unmistakably a dwarf. He came forward and clapped Colin on the shoulder, and Colin rocked under the blow.

'And it is I, Uthecar Hornskin, that love you for it! Hey now! Will his mightiness come down out of yon tree and speak with his friends?' The white figure in the tree did not move: he seemed not to hear what was said. 'I am thinking there is more need of elf-shot in other parts of the wood this night than here! I see Albanac coming, and he in no quiet mood!'

The dwarf looked down the path beyond Colin and Susan. They could not see far in the dark, but they heard the faint sound of hoofs pounding towards them. Nearer and louder they grew, and then out of the night came a black horse, wild-eyed and sweating, and halted in a spray of sand. Its rider, a tall man, himself clothed in black, called up into the tree. 'My lord Atlendor! We have found it, but it is free of the wood to the south, and moving too fast for me. Ermid son of Erbin, Riogan son of Moren, and Anwas the Winged, with half their can-trefs, have it in sight, but they are not enough. Hurry!' His straight hair hung black upon his shoulders, gold glinted at his ear, and his eyes were like burning ice. A deep-crowned, wide-brimmed hat was on his head, and about his shoulders was a cloak fastened with a silver buckle.

'I go. Albanac shall teach my will to these folk.' The elf ran lightly along the birch trunk and disappeared into the crown. There was a rush of white in the surrounding trees, like swirling snow, and a noise like wind in the branches.

For some time nobody spoke. The dwarf gave the impression that he was enjoying the situation and was happy to let others make the next move; the man called Albanac looked at the children; and Colin and Susan were recovering from their surprise, and taking in the fact that they were back in the world of Magic – by accident, it seemed; and now that they were back, they remembered that this was a world of deep shadows as well as of enchantment.

They had been walking into it ever since they reached the quarry. If they could have recognised this atmosphere for what it was, the successive shocks of elf, dwarf, and rider would not have been so breathless.

'I think now,' said Albanac, 'that the matter is out of Cadellin's hands.'

'What do you mean?' said Colin. 'And what's all this about?'

'As for what I mean, that will take some telling, and what it is about is the same thing. And the place for it all is Fundindelve, so let us go together.'

'Is there not more urgent business in the wood this night?' said Uthecar.

'Nothing that we can do,' said Albanac. 'The speed and the eyes of elves are the only hope, and I fear they will not be enough.'

He dismounted from his horse, and walked with the children and the dwarf back along the path. But after a little while, Susan noticed that they were not making for the Holywell.

'Wouldn't it be quicker that way?' she said, pointing to their left.

'It would,' said Albanac, 'but this way the path is broader, which is a good thing this night.'

They came to a wide expanse of stone and sand which spilled down the face of the Edge. This was Stormy Point, a place of fine views in daylight, but now it was friendless. From here they crossed over the rocks to Saddlebole, which was a spur of the hill jutting into the plain, and half-way along this stood a tall boulder.

'Will you open the gates, Susan?' said Albanac.

'But I can't,' said Susan. 'I've tried often enough.'

'Colin,' said Albanac, 'will you put your right hand to the rock, and say the word "Emalagra"?'

'What, like this?'

'Yes.'

'Emalagra?'

'Again.'

'Emalagra! *Emalagra!*'

Nothing happened. Colin stood back, looking foolish.

'Now Susan,' said Albanac.

Susan stepped up to the boulder, and put her right hand against it.

'Emalagra. See? It's no good. I've tried every —'

A crack appeared in the rock; it grew wider, revealing a pair of iron gates, and beyond these a tunnel lit by a blue light.

CHAPTER 4

The Brollachan

'Will you open the gates?' said Albanac.

Susan stretched out her hand, and touched the iron gates. They swung open.

'Quickly now,' said Uthecar. 'It is a healthier night within than without.'

He hurried the children through the gates, and the rock closed after them the moment they were all inside.

'Why did they open? They wouldn't before,' said Susan.

'Because you spoke the word, and for another reason that we shall talk about,' said Albanac.

They went with Albanac down the paths of Fundindelve. Tunnel entered cave, and cave gave way to tunnel: caves, and tunnels, each different and the same: there seemed to be no end.

As they went deeper the blue light grew pale and strong, and by this the children knew that they were nearing the Cave of the Sleepers, for whose sake the old dwarf-mine of Fundindelve had been charged with the greatest magic of an age, and its guardian was Cadellin Silverbrow. Here in this cave, waiting through the centuries for the day when Cadellin should rouse him from his enchanted sleep to fight the last battle of the world, lay a king, surrounded by his knights, each with his milk-white mare.

The children looked about them, at the cold flames, now white in the core of the magic, flickering over the silver armour, at the horses, and the men, and listened to the muted, echoing murmur of their breathing, the beating of the heart of Fundindelve.

From the Cave of the Sleepers the way led uphill, by more tunnels, by stark, high-arching bridges over unknown depths, along narrow paths in the roofs of caves, across vaulted plains of sand, to the furthest caverns of the mine. And finally they came to a small cave close behind the Holywell that the wizard used for his quarters. In it were a few chairs, a long table, and a bed of skins.

'Where's Cadellin?' said Susan.

'He will be with the lios-alfar, the elves,' said Albanac. 'Many of them are ill of the smoke-sickness : but until he comes, rest you here. There is doubtless much you would know.'

'There certainly is!' said Colin. 'Who was that shooting arrows at us?'

'The elf-lord, Atlendor son of Naf : he needs your help.'

'*Needs our help?*' said Colin. 'He went a funny way about getting it!'

'But I never thought elves would be like *that*!' said Susan.

'No,' said Albanac. 'You are both too hasty. Remember, he is under fear at this time. Danger besets him; he is tired, alone – and he is a king. Remember, too, that no elf has a natural love of men; for it is the dirt and ugliness and unclean air that men have worshipped these two hundred years that have driven the lios-alfar to the trackless places and the broken lands. You should see the smoke-sickness in the elves of Talebolion and Sinadon. You should hear it in their lungs. That is what men have done.'

'But how *can* we help?' said Susan.

'I will show you,' said Albanac. 'Cadellin has spoken against this for many days, and he has good reason, but now you are here, and I think we must tell you what is wrong.

'In brief, it is this. There is something hiding in the

dead wastes of the Northland, in far Prydein where the last kingdom of the elves has been made. For a long while now the numbers of the lios-alfar have been growing less – not through the smoke-sickness, as is happening in the west, but for some cause that we have not found. Elves vanish. They go without a sign. At first it was by ones and twos, but not long since a whole cantref, the cantref of Grannos, was lost, horses and weapons: not an arrow was seen. Some great wrong is at work, and to find it, and destroy it, Atlendor is bringing his people to him from the south and the west, gathering what magic he can. Susan, will you let him take the Mark of Fohla?'

'What's that?' said Susan.

'It is the bracelet that Angharad Goldenhand gave to you.'

'*This?*' said Susan. 'I didn't know it had a name. What good is it to Atlendor?'

'I do not know,' said Albanac. 'But any magic may help him – and you have magic there. Did you not open the gates?'

Susan looked at the band of ancient silver that she wore on her wrist. It was all she had brought with her out of the wreckage of their last encounter with this world, and it had been given to her, on a night of danger and enchantment, by Angharad Goldenhand, the Lady of the Lake. Susan did not know the meaning of the heavy letters that were traced in black, in a forgotten script, upon the silver, yet she knew that it was no ordinary bracelet, and she did not wear it lightly.

'Why is it called that?' said Susan.

'There are tales,' said Albanac, 'that I have only dimly heard about these things, yet I know that the Marks of Fohla are from the early magic of the world, and this is the first that I have ever seen, and I cannot tell its use. But will you give it to Atlendor?'

'I can't,' said Susan.

'But the elves may be destroyed for lack of the Mark!' said Albanac. 'Will you fail them when they most need help?'

'Of course I'll help,' said Susan. 'It's just that Angharad told me I must always look after my bracelet, though she didn't say why: but if Atlendor needs it, I'll go back with him.'

At this, Uthecar laughed, but Albanac's face was troubled.

'You have me there,' he said. 'Atlendor will not like this. But wait: is he to know? I do not want to burden him with fresh troubles if they can be avoided. Perhaps this would be of no use to Atlendor, but let me take it to him, Susan, so that he can try its powers. If they are deaf to him he will accept your provision more easily.'

'And why should himself not be away beyond Bannawg sooner than the fox to the wood, and the Mark with him?' said Uthecar.

'You do not know the lios-alfar, Hornskin,' said Albanac. 'I give you my word that there will be no deceit.'

'Then another word shall go into Cadellin's ear,' said Uthecar, 'lest Atlendor should think black danger merits black deed. None of the lios-alfar will leave Fundindelve if Cadellin bids them stay.'

'No,' said Susan. 'I trust you. And I think I trust Atlendor. Here you are: let him see what he can do with it. But please don't keep it any longer than you need.'

'Thank you,' said Albanac. 'You will not be sorry.'

'Let us hope so,' said Uthecar. He did not look at all happy. 'But from what I have heard of you, I am thinking you are not wise to put off your armour. The Morrigan does not forget, and she does not forgive.'

'The Morrigan?' said Colin. 'Where? Is she after us again?'

Although the children had first crossed this woman in

her human shape, they ha
more to her than her un
gan, leader of the wi
and above that, she c
brew hate from the a
strength. But mainly thr
had been broken by Cadel
not been certain that she he
truction that had overwhelmed h

'The morthbrood is scattered,' s   ac, 'but she
has been seen. You had best ask him   o brought word
of her.' He nodded towards Uthecar. 'This honey-natured
dwarf from beyond Minith Bannawg in the Northland.'

'Why? Have you seen her?' said Colin.

'Have I not!' said the dwarf. 'Are you all wanting to
know? Well then, here is the tale.

'On my way south I came to the hill of the Black
Fernbrake in Prydein, and a storm followed me. So I was
looking for rocks and heather to make a shelter for the
night. I saw a round, brown stone, as if it were set apart
from other stones, and I put my arms about it to lift it
up – and oh, king of the sun and of the moon, and of the
bright and fragrant stars! the stone put arms about my
neck, and was throttling the life of me!

'Ask not how, for I cannot say, but I plucked myself
free; and then the stone was the Morrigan! I sprang at
her with my sword, and though she took out my eye, I
took off her head, and the Black Fernbrake's sides called
to her screech.

'But the head leapt a hard, round leap to the neck
again, and she came at me loathingly, and I was much
in fear of her. Three times we fought, and three times I
lifted her head, and three times she was whole again, and
I was near death with pain and faintness.

'So once more I set iron to her shoulders, but when the
head was making for the trunk I put my sword on the

lished 1963 by William Collins Sons
14 St James's Place, London SW1
First published in Lions 1972
Sixth Impression 1977
© Alan Garner 1963

neck, and the head played "gliong" on the blade, and sprang up to the skies. Then it began to fall, and I saw that it was aiming at me, so I stepped aside, and it went six feet into the ground with the force it had. Was that not the head! Then I heard stones crunching, and a chewing, and a gnawing, and a gnashing, so I thought it was time for me to take my legs along with me, and I went on through the night and the winnowing and the snow in it.'

They were waiting now for the wizard to come. And while they waited, Uthecar saw to it that talk never flagged.

He told how Albanac had met him one day, and had spoken of a rumour that something had come out of the ground near Fundindelve and was being hunted by Cadellin Silverbrow. Having himself been idle too long, Uthecar had decided to make the journey south from Minith Bannawg, in the hope that Cadellin would be glad of his help. He was not disappointed. The matter was greater than he thought —

Long ago, one of the old mischiefs of the world had brought fear to the plain, but it had been caught, and imprisoned in a pit at the foot of the Edge. Centuries later, through the foolishness of men, it had escaped, and was taken at heavy cost. Albanac's news was that men had loosed the evil a second time.

'And there was no knowing in the hard, shrivelling world,' said Uthecar, 'where we might find the Brollachan again.'

The Brollachan. 'Now the Brollachan,' said Uthecar, 'has eyes and a mouth, and it has no speech, and alas no shape.' It was beyond comprehension. Yet the shadow that rose in Susan's mind as the dwarf spoke seemed to her to darken the cave.

Shortly after this, Cadellin arrived. His shoulders were bowed, his weight leaning on the staff in his hand. When he saw the children a frown grew in the lines about his eyes.

'Colin? Susan? I am glad to see you; but why are you here? Albanac, why have you gone behind me to do this?'

'It is not quite so, Cadellin,' said Albanac. 'But first, what of the lios-alfar?'

'The elves of Dinsel and Talebolion will be slow to heal,' said Cadellin. 'These that have come from Sinadon are stronger, but the smoke-sickness is on them, and some I fear are beyond my hand.

'Now tell me what has brought you here.'

He spoke to the children.

'We were – stopped by Atlendor – the elf – and then Uthecar and Albanac came,' said Susan, 'and we've just heard about the elves.'

'Do you think badly of Atlendor,' said Albanac. 'He is hard-pressed. But Susan has given us hope: I have the Mark of Fohla here.'

Cadellin looked at Susan. 'I – am glad,' he said. 'It is noble, Susan. But is it wise? Oh, you must think I have the destruction of elves at heart! But the Morrigan —'

'We have spoken of her,' said Albanac quickly. 'The bracelet will not be with me for long, and I do not think that witch-queen will come south yet awhile. She will have to be much stronger before she dare move openly, and she does not feel safe even beyond Minith Bannawg, if Hornskin's tale speaks true. Why else the shape-shifting among rocks unless she fears pursuit?'

'That is so,' agreed Cadellin. 'I know I am too cautious. Yet still I do not like to see these children brought even to the threshold of danger – no, Susan, do not be angry. It is not your age but your humanity that gives me unrest. It is against my wishes that you are here now.'

'But *why*?' cried Susan.

'Why do you think men know us only in legend?' said Cadellin. 'We do not have to avoid you for our safety, as elves must, but rather for your own. It has not always been so. Once we were close; but some little time before the elves were driven away, a change came over you. You found the world easier to master by hands alone: things became more than thoughts with you, and you called it an Age of Reason.

'Now with us the opposite holds true, so that in our affairs you are weakest where you should be strong, and there is danger for you not only from evil, but from other matters we touch upon. These may not be evil, but they are wild forces, which could destroy one not well acquainted with such things.

'For these reasons we withdrew from mankind, and became a memory, and, with the years, a superstition, ghosts and terrors for a winter's night, and later a mockery and a disbelief.

'That is why I must appear so hard: do you understand?'

'I – think so,' said Susan. 'Most of it, anyway.'

'But if you cut yourself off all that while ago,' said Colin, 'how is it that you talk as we do?'

'But we do not,' said the wizard. 'We use the Common Tongue now because you are here. Among ourselves there are many languages. And have you not noticed that there are some of us stranger to the Tongue than others? The elves have avoided men most completely. They speak the Tongue much as they last heard it, and that not well. The rest – I, the dwarfs, and a few more – have heard it through the years, and know it better than do the elves, though we cannot master your later speed and shortness. Albanac sees most of men, and *he* is often lost, but since they think him mad it is of no account.'

Colin and Susan did not stay long in the cave: the mood of the evening remained uneasy and it was obvious that Cadellin had more on his mind than had been said. A little after seven o'clock they walked up the short tunnel that led from the cave to the Holywell. The wizard touched the rock with his staff, and the cliff opened.

Uthecar went with the children all the way to the farm, turning back only at the gate. Colin and Susan were aware of his eyes ranging continually backwards and forwards, around and about.

'What's the matter?' said Susan. 'What are you looking for?'

'Something I hope I shall not be finding,' said Uthecar. 'You may have noticed that the woods were not empty this night. We were close on the Brollachan, and it is far from here that I hope it is just now.'

'But how could you see it, whatever it is?' said Colin. 'It's pitch dark tonight.'

'You must know the eyes of a dwarf are born to darkness,' said Uthecar. 'But even you would see the Brollachan, though the night were as black as a wolf's throat; for no matter how black the night, the Brollachan is blacker than that.'

This stopped conversation for the rest of the journey. But when they reached Highmost Redmanhey, Susan said, 'Uthecar, what's wrong with the elves? I – don't mean to be rude, but I've always imagined them to be the – well, the "best" of your people.'

'Ha!' said Uthecar. 'They would agreee with you! And few would gainsay them. You must judge for yourselves. But I will say this of the lios-alfar; they are merciless without kindliness, and there are things incomprehensible about them.'

CHAPTER 5

'To a Woman yt was Dumpe'

About half a mile from Highmost Redmanhey, round the shoulder of Clinton hill, there is a disused and flooded quarry. Where the sides are not cliffs, wooded slopes drop steeply. A broken wind pump creaks, and a forgotten path runs nowhere into the brambles. In sunlight it is a forlorn place, forlorn as nothing but deserted machinery can be; but when the sun goes in, the air is charged with a different feeling. The water is sombre under its brows of cliff, and the trees crowd down to drink, the pump sneers; lonely, green-hued, dark.

But peaceful, thought Susan, and that's something.

There had been no peace at the farm since their return. Two days of talk from Colin, and the silences made heavy by the Mossocks' uneasiness. For Bess and Gowther knew of the children's past involvement with magic, and they were as troubled by this mixing of the two worlds as Cadellin had been.

The weather did not help. The air was still, moist, too warm for the beginning of winter.

Susan had felt that she must go away to relax; so that afternoon she had left Colin and had come to the quarry. She stood on the edge of a slab of rock that stretched into the water, and lost herself in the grey shadows of fish. She was there a long time, slowly unwinding the tensions of the days: and then a noise made her look up.

'Hallo. Who are you?'

A small black pony was standing at the edge of the water on the other side of the quarry.

'What are you doing here?'

The pony tossed its mane, and snorted.

'Come on, then! Here, boy!'

The pony looked hard at Susan, flicked its tail, then turned and disappeared among the trees.

'Oh, well— I wonder what the time is.' Susan climbed up the slope out of the quarry and into the field. She walked round to the wood on the far side, and whistled, but nothing happened. 'Here, boy! Here, boy! Oh don't, then; I'm – oh!'

The pony was standing right behind her.

'You made me jump! Where've you been?'

Susan fondled the pony's ears. It seemed to like that, for it thrust its head into her shoulder, and closed its velvet-black eyes.

'Steady! You'll knock me over.'

For several minutes she stroked its neck, then reluctantly she pushed it away. 'I must go now. I'll come and see you tomorrow.' The pony trotted after her. 'No, go back. You can't come.' But the pony followed Susan all the way across the field, butting her gently with its head and nibbling at her ears. And when she came to climb through the fence into the next field, it put itself between her and the fence, and pushed sideways with its sleek belly.

'What do you want?'

Push.

'I've nothing for you.'

Push.

'What *is* it?'

Push.

'Do you want me to ride? That's it, isn't it? Stand still, then. There. Good boy. You *have* got a long back, haven't you? There. Now – woa! Steady!'

The moment Susan was astride, the pony wheeled round and set off at full gallop towards the quarry. Susan grabbed the mane with both hands.

'Hey! Stop!'

They were heading straight for the barbed wire at the top of the cliff above the deepest part of the quarry.

'No! Stop!'

The pony turned its head and looked at Susan. Its foaming lips curled back in a grin, and the velvet was gone from the eye: in the heart of the black pupil was a red flame.

'*No!*' Susan screamed.

Faster and faster they went. The edge of the cliff cut a hard line against the sky. Susan tried to throw herself from the pony's back, but her fingers seemed to be entangled in the mane, and her legs clung to the ribs.

'*No! No! No! No!*'

The pony soared over the fence, and plunged past smooth sandstone down to the water. The splash echoed between the walls, waves slapped the rock, there were some bubbles: the quarry was silent under the heavy sky.

'I'm not waiting any longer,' said Bess. 'Susan mun get her own tea when she comes in.'

'Ay, let's be doing,' said Gowther. 'Theer's one or two things to be seen to before it rains, and it conner be far off now: summat's got to bust soon.'

'I'll be glad when it does,' said Bess. 'I conner get my breath today. Did Susan say she'd be late?'

'No,' said Colin, 'but you know what she is. And she hadn't a watch with her.'

They sat down at the table, and ate without talking. The only sounds were the breathing of Bess and Gowther, the ticking of the clock, the idiot buzz of two winter-drugged flies that circled endlessly under the beams. The sky bore down on the farm-house, squeezing the people in it like apples in a press.

'We're for it, reet enough,' said Gowther. 'And Susan had best hurry if she dunner want a soaking. She ought to be here by now. Wheer was she for, Colin? Eh up! What's getten into him?' Scamp, the Mossocks' lurcher, had begun to bark wildly somewhere close. Gowther put his head out of the window. 'That'll do! Hey!

'Now then, what was I saying? Oh ay; Susan. Do you know wheer she's gone?'

'She said she was going to the quarry for some peace and quiet – I've been getting on her nerves, she said.'

'What? Hayman's quarry? You should have said earlier, Colin. It's a dangerous — oh, drat the dog! Hey! Scamp! That's enough! Do you hear?'

'Oh!' said Bess. 'Whatever's to do with you? Wheer've you been?'

Susan was standing in the doorway, looking pale and dazed. Her hair was thick with mud, and a pool of water was gathering at her feet.

'The quarry!' said Gowther. 'She mum have fallen in! What were you thinking of, Susan, to go and do that?'

'Bath and bed,' said Bess, 'and then we'll see what's what. Eh dear!'

She took Susan by the arm, and bustled her out of sight.

'Goodness knows what happened,' said Bess when she came downstairs half an hour later. 'Her hair was full of sand and weed. But I couldner get a word out of her: she seems mazed, or summat. Hapen she'll be better for a sleep: I've put a couple of hot-water bottles in her bed, and she looked as though she'd drop off any minute when I left her.'

The storm battered the house, and filled the rooms with currents of air, making the lamps roar. It had come soon after nightfall, and with it a release of tension. The house was now a refuge, and not a prison. Colin, once the immediate anxiety for Susan had been allayed,

settled down to spend the evening with his favourite
book.

This was a musty, old ledger, covered with brown
suède. Over a hundred years ago, one of the rectors of
Alderley had copied into it a varied series of documents
relating to the parish. The book had been in Gowther's
family longer than he could say, and although he had
never found the patience to decipher the crabbed hand-
writing, he treasured the book as a link with a time that
had passed. But Colin was fascinated by the anecdotes,
details of court leets, surveys of the parish, manorial
grants, and family histories that filled the book. There
was always something absurd to be found, if you had
Colin's sense of humour.

The page that held him now was headed:

EXTRACTS: CH: WARDENS' ACCS. 1617

A true and perfect account of all such Sumes of
Money as I, John Henshaw of ye Butts, Churchwar-
den of Neither Alderley and for ye parish of Alderley
have received and likewise disburst since my first
entrance into Office untill this present day being ye
28 May Anno Di. 1618.

	£	s.	d.
Imprimis Payed for Ale for ye Ringers and oure Selves	0	3	2
Item to John Wych his bill for a new Sally Poll	0	2	0
Item to a man yt had his tongue cut out by ye Turks	0	0	2
Item to Philip Lea half his bill for walking	0	1	6
Item to a pretended Irish gentleman	0	1	3
Item spent for cluckin to make nets	0	1	8
Item to a woman yt was dumpe	0	0	6

Item spent when I did goe throw ye town to
    warne those to bring in ye wrishes yt had
    neglected on ye wrish burying day   o o 4
Item given to a Majer yt had been taken by
    ye French and was runeated by them   o i o
Item payed to Mr. Hollinshead for warrants
    to punish ye boys' Immoralities   o o 8

But the next entry took all the laughter from Colin's
face. He read it through twice.

'Gowther!'

'Ay?'

'Listen to this: it's part of the churchwardens'
accounts for 1617.

    ' "Item spent at Street Lane Ends when Mr. Hollins-
head and Mr. Wright were at Paynes to confine ye
devil yt was fownde at ye Ale house when ye new
pipe was being put down and it did break into ye
Pitt." '

'Do you think it's the hole at the Trafford?'

Gowther frowned. 'Ay, I'd say it is, what with the
pipe, and all. That side of Alderley near the Trafford
used to be called Street Lane Ends, and I've heard tell of a
pub theer before the Trafford was built. Sixteen-seven-
teen, is it? It conner be part of the mines, then. They
didner come that way until about two hundred years
back, when West Mine was started. So it looks as though
it was the well of the owd pub, dunner it?'

'But it couldn't be,' said Colin. 'It was called "ye Pitt",
and by the sound of it, they didn't know it was there. So
what is it?'

'Nay, dunner ask me,' said Gowther. 'And who are
yon Hollinshead and Wright?'

'They're often mentioned in here,' said Colin. 'I think

they were the priests at Alderley and Wilmslow. I'd like to know more about this "devil".'

'I dunner reckon much on that,' said Gowther. 'They were a superstitious lot in them days. As a matter of fact, I was talking to Jack Wrigley yesterday – he's the feller as put his pickaxe through the slab – and he said that when he was looking to see what he'd got, he heard a rum kind of bubbling sound that put the wind up him a bit, but he thinks it was summat to do with air pressure. Happen yon's what the parsons took for Owd Nick.'

'I dunner like it,' said Bess from the doorway. She had just come downstairs. 'Susan's not spoken yet, and she's as cold as a frog. And I conner think wheer all the sand's coming from – her hair's still full of it – and everything's wringing wet. Still, that's not surprising with two hot-water bottles, I suppose. But theer's summat wrong; she's lying theer staring at nowt, and her eyes are a bit queer.'

'Mun I go for the doctor, do you think?' said Gowther.

'What? In this rain? And it's nearly ten o'clock. Nay, lad, she inner that bad. But if things are no different in the morning, we'll have the doctor in sharpish.'

'But what if she's getten concussion, or summat like that?' said Gowther.

'It's more like shock, I reckon,' said Bess. 'Theer's no bruises or lumps as I con see, and either way, she's in the best place for her. You'd not get much thanks from the doctor for dragging him up here in this. We'll see how she is for a good neet's rest.'

Bess, like many country-women of her age, could not shake off her unreasoned fear of medical men.

Colin never knew what woke him. He lay on his back and stared at the moonlight. He had woken suddenly and completely, with no buffer of drowsiness to take the shock. His senses were needle-pointed, he was aware of every detail of the room, the pools of light and darkness shouted at him.

He got out of bed, and went to the window. It was a clear night, the air cold and sweet after the storm: the moon cast hard shadows over the farmyard. Scamp lay by the barn door, his head between his paws. Then Colin saw something move. He saw it only out of the corner of his eye, and it was gone in a moment, but he was never in any doubt: a shadow had slipped across the patch of moonlight that lay between the end of the house and the gate that led to the Riddings, the steep hill-field behind the farm.

'Hey! Scamp!' whispered Colin. The dog did not move. 'Hey! Wake up!' Scamp whined softly, and gave a muted yelp. 'Come on! Fetch him!' Scamp whined again, then crawled, barely raising his belly from the floor, into the barn. 'What on earth? Hey!' But Scamp would not come.

Colin pulled on his shirt and trousers over his pyjamas, and jammed his feet into a pair of shoes, before going to wake Gowther. But when he came to Susan's door he paused, and, for no reason that he could explain, opened the door. The bed was empty, the window open.

Colin tiptoed downstairs and groped his way to the door. It was still bolted. Had Susan dropped nine feet to the cobbles? He eased the bolts, and stepped outside, and as he looked he saw a thin silhouette pass over the sky-line of the Riddings.

He struggled up the hill as fast as he could, but it was some time before he spotted the figure again, now moving across Clinton hill, a quarter of a mile away.

Colin ran: and by the time he stood up at the top of Clinton hill he had halved the lead that Susan had gained. For it was undoubtedly Susan. She was wearing her pyjamas, and she seemed to glide smoothly over the ground, giving a strange impression that she was running, though her movements were those of walking. Straight ahead of her were the dark tops of the trees in the quarry.

'Sue!' No, wait. That's dangerous. She's sleep-walking. But she's heading for the quarry.

Colin ran as hard as he had ever run. Once he was off the hill-top the uneven ground hid Susan, but he knew the general direction. He came to the fence that stood on the edge of the highest cliff and looked around while he recovered his breath.

The moon showed all the hill-side and much of the quarry: the pump-tower gleamed, and the vanes turned. But Susan was nowhere to be seen. Colin leant against a fence-stump. She ought to be in sight: he could not have overtaken her: she must have reached here. Colin searched the sides of the quarry with his eyes, and looked at the smooth black mirror of the water. He was frightened. Where was she?

Then he cried out his fear as something slithered over his shoe and plucked at his ankle. He started back, and looked down. It was a hand. A ledge of earth, inches wide, ran along the other side of the fence and crumbled away to the rock face a few feet below: then the drop was sheer to the tarn-like water. The hand now clutched the ledge.

'Sue!'

He stretched over the barbed wire. She was right below him, spreadeagled between the ledge and the cliff proper, her pale face turned up to his.

'Hang on! Oh, hang on!'

Colin threw himself flat on the ground, wrapped one arm round the stump, thrust the other under the wire, and grabbed at the hand. But though it looked like a hand, it felt like a hoof.

The wire tore Colin's sleeve as he shouted and snatched his arm away. Then, as Susan's face rose above the ledge, a foot from his own, and he saw the light that glowed in her eyes, Colin abandoned reason, thought. He shot backwards from the ledge, crouched, stumbled, fled. He looked back only once, and it seemed that out of the quarry a formless shadow was rising into the sky. Behind him the stars went out, but in their place were two red stars, unwinking, and close together.

Colin sped along the hill, vaulting fences, throwing himself over hedges, and plunging down the Riddings to the farm-house. As he fumbled with the door, the moon was hidden, and darkness slid over the white walls. Colin turned. '*Esenaroth! Esenaroth!*' he cried. The words came to him and were torn from his lips independent of his will, and he heard them from a distance, as though they were from another's mouth. They burned like silver fire in his brain, sanctuary in the blackness that filled the world.

CHAPTER 6

Old Evil

'I think we mun have the doctor,' said Bess. 'She's wet
through again – it conner be healthy. And that blessed
sand! Her hair's still full of it.'

'Reet,' said Gowther. 'I'll get Prince ready, and then I'll
go and ring him up.'

Colin ate his breakfast mechanically. Bess and
Gowther's voices passed over him. He had to do something, but he did not know what he could do.

He had been woken by Scamp's warm tongue on his
face. It must have been about six o'clock in the morning: he was huddled on the doorstep, stiff with cold. He
heard Gowther clump downstairs into the kitchen. Colin
wondered if he should tell him what had happened, but
it was not clear in his own head: he had to have time to
think. So he tucked his pyjamas out of sight, and went to
light the lamps for milking.

After breakfast Colin still had reached no decision. He
went upstairs and changed his clothes. Susan's door was
ajar. He made himself go into the room. She lay in bed,
her eyes half-closed, and when she saw Colin she smiled.

He went down to the kitchen, and found it empty. Bess
was feeding the hens, and Gowther was in the stable
with Prince. Colin was alone in the house with – what?
He needed help, and Fundindelve was his only hope. He
went into the yard, frightened, desperate, and then
almost sobbing with relief, for Albanac was striding
down the Riddings, the sun sparkling on his silver
buckles and sword, his cloak swelling behind him in the
wind.

Colin ran towards him and they met at the foot of the hill.

'Albanac! Albanac!'

'Why, what is it? Colin, are you well?'

'It's Sue!'

'*What?*' Albanac took Colin by the shoulders and looked hard into his eyes. 'Where is she?'

'I don't know – she's in bed – no – I mean – you must listen!'

'I am listening, but I do not follow you. Now tell me what is wrong.'

'I'm sorry,' said Colin. He paused, and then began. As he spoke, Albanac's face grew lined and tense, his eyes were like blue diamonds. When Colin started to describe how he had followed Susan to the quarry Albanac interrupted him.

'Can we be seen from her window?'

'No – well, just about. It's that end window at the front.'

'Then I would not be here.'

They moved round until the gable end of the house hid them from any windows.

'Now go on.'

When the story was finished Albanac laughed bitterly. 'Ha! This is matter indeed. So near, after all. But come, we must act before the chance is lost.'

'Why? What —?'

'Listen. Can we enter the house without being seen from the window?'

'Ye-es.'

'Good. I think I have not the power to do what should be done, but we must think first of Susan. Now mark what I say: we must not speak when we are nearer the house.

'Lead me to the room. I shall make little sound, but

you must walk as though you had no guile. Go to the window and open it : then we shall see.'

Colin paused with his hand on the latch and looked over his shoulder. Albanac stood at the top of the stairs; he nodded. Colin opened the door.

Susan lay there, staring. Colin crossed to the window and unlatched it. At the sound, Albanac stepped into the room : he held the Mark of Fohla, open, in his hand. Susan snarled, her eyes flashing wide, and tore the blankets from her, but Albanac threw himself across the room and on to the bed, striking Susan under the chin with his shoulder and pinning her arm beneath him while he locked the bracelet about her wrist. Then, as quickly, he sprang back to the door and drew his sword.

'Colin! Outside!'

'What have you done?' cried Colin. 'What's happening?'

Albanac's hand bit into his shoulder and flung him out of the room. Albanac jumped after him and slammed the door shut.

'Alb—'

'Quiet!' said Albanac, and his voice was iron. 'When she is free, then must we beware. Let us hope the bracelet causes such pain that escape means more than vengeance.'

They stood motionless, rigid; the only sound was the creaking of Susan's bed; then that stopped. Silence.

'Albanac! *Look!*'

A black coil of smoke was sliding under the door. It rolled forward on to the floor, where it gathered in an unstable pyramid, which grew.

'If you would live,' whispered Albanac, 'stay by me!'

The pyramid was now some three feet high. Near the top glowed two red eyes : near the base was what could have been a shadowy mouth, or a shallow beak. Then the thing began to grow. It grew in many directions, like a balloon, and it grew in spasms, with moments of rest in between.

Albanac raised his sword, and spoke in a hard, clear voice.

'Power of wind have I over thee.

'Power of wrath have I over thee.

'Power of fire have I over thee.

'Power of thunder have I over thee.

'Power of lightning have I over thee.'

The pyramid now filled the house: it was no longer a pyramid: it was everything – a universal darkness in which there were two flat discs, the colour of blood, and a ribbon of blue fire that was Albanac's sword.

'Power of storms have I over thee.

'Power of moon have I over thee.

'Power of sun have I over thee.

'Power of stars have I over thee.'

The blank eyes swam closer, now as big as plates, and the darkness began to pulse, and Colin gripped Albanac's cloak like a drowning man; for the pulse was the rhythm of his heartbeats, and he could not tell where he ended and the darkness began.

'Power of the – heavens – and – of the worlds – have I – over – thee.

'Power – power – *I cannot hold it!*'

Albanac lifted his sword above his head with both hands, and drove it down into the blackness between the eyes.

'*Eson! Eson! Emaris!*'

There was a glare of light, and a tearing crash. The house quivered, the door burst inwards, a wind shrieked through the room, and all was quiet. Albanac and Colin slowly raised their heads from the floor, and pulled themselves upright against the doorposts.

The room was smashed and the furniture scattered, the window frame had splintered from the wall. Albanac's sword was in pieces. Only Susan was undisturbed: she lay quietly, breathing deeply, fast asleep. Colin went to the bed and looked down at her.

'Sue. It *is* – Sue?'

Albanac nodded.

There were voices outside in the yard, then heavy footsteps on the stairs, and Gowther stood in the doorway.

'What —?'

Bess appeared behind him.

'Who —? Oh dear! Oh dear! Oh! Oh! Oh! Oh!'

'Howd thy noise, lass,' said Gowther. He looked at Albanac. 'Now, maister, what's all this about?'

'That, farmer Mossock, was the Brollachan.'

'The *what*?'

'Ay, and there is work to be done, and swiftly – though I doubt if we shall pick up the trail. I must go to Fundindelve, but I shall be back. Let Susan sleep, and see to it that the bracelet stays on her wrist, then she will be safe.'

'I was just on my way for the doctor,' said Gowther.

'No!' Albanac turned on Gowther. 'You must not do that. Let Cadellin see her first.'

'But —'

'Believe me! You may do harm. This is no business for men.'

'No? Happen you're reet – and happen you're not. She's looking better, I'll grant you. All reet: we'll wait on a bit: but you'd best be sharp.'

'Thank you, farmer Mossock.'

Albanac ran from the house, and they watched him till he crossed over the Riddings, and not a word was spoken.

Words were spoken later. Bess and Gowther listened to Colin's story, and they accepted it. They had to. The wrecked bedroom was too compelling a witness.

They had spent several hours repairing what they could and patching up the rest. Through it all Susan had slept without a break : for Bess it was the one consolation of the day. It was a restful sleep, not the dead, withdrawn, near-coma that had troubled Bess more than she would admit. Susan was still pale, but it was a healthy paleness compared with what had gone before.

The tap at the door was so light that if they had not been sitting quietly at the table over a late tea they would not have heard it.

'Was that someone knocking?' said Gowther.

'I think it was,' said Bess. 'But I might be wrong?'

'Hallo,' said Gowther. 'Who is it?'

'Albanac.'

'Oh!' Gowther crossed to the door. 'Er – ay, come in.'

Albanac entered the kitchen, followed by Uthecar and Cadellin. The wizard stooped under the beams : when he stood upright his head could not be seen.

'Er – take a seat, will you?' said Gowther.

'Thank you,' said Cadellin. 'How is Susan?'

'Oh, she's still asleep; and we've not tried to wake her, seeing how Albanac here said we should leave her be, but she's looking much better – else we'd have had the doctor to her by now, I'll tell thee.'

'*Still* sleeping?' said Cadellin.

'You have not taken the bracelet from her wrist?' said Albanac sharply.

'No.'

'I think we must see her,' said Cadellin.

'What's wrong?' said Colin. 'Why are you all looking

so grim?'

'I hope there is nothing wrong,' said the wizard. 'Albanac came in time, and it is well he did. The Brollachan does not willingly leave a body until it is beyond repair. Susan has escaped – I hope without injury – but it would be wise for us to see her.'

'Look,' said Bess, who had been sitting agape since the moment she saw the wizard, 'I dunner pretend to follow this here, but if Susan needs attention, the doctor's the mon to do it. I've said so all along.'

'Ay,' said Gowther; 'you con go and have a look at her, if you wish, but that's all. After what she seems to have been through, the less mumbo-jumbo theer is about her the better. We're having the doctor in tomorrow to give her a good overhauling, and then we'll see.'

'Hm,' said Cadellin.

They went upstairs. Susan was still asleep. Cadellin looked at her.

'It is safe to wake her, farmer Mossock. Her body is not hurt, and she is rested.'

Bess leant over the bed and shook Susan gently. 'Susan. Come on, love: it's time to wake up.' Susan did not move. Bess shook her harder. 'Come on, lass. Wake up.' But Susan gave no signs of waking, no matter how Bess tried.

'Mistress Mossock,' said Cadellin softly, 'let me try.'

Bess stepped back, and the wizard took hold of Susan's wrist and felt her pulse, then he lifted her eyelid. 'Hm.' He put his left hand on her brow, and closed his eyes. The room was silent. A minute, two minutes passed.

'Is she all right?' said Colin. The wizard did not reply. He seemed to be scarcely breathing. 'Cadellin!'

'Here! What's going on?' said Gowther, and made to grab Cadellin's arm. But Albanac stepped in front of him.

'No, farmer Mossock: do not interfere.'

As he spoke, Cadellin opened his eyes. 'She is not here. She is lost to us.'

'*What?*' cried Colin. 'What do you mean? She's not dead. She can't be! Look! She's only asleep!'

'Her body sleeps,' said Cadellin. 'Let us leave her now : there is something you must know.'

CHAPTER 7

Old Magic

'The Brollachan,' said Albanac, 'has no shape. It must take that of others. But no mortal frame can bear it for long: it is too fierce a tenant. Soon the body stretches, warps, becomes the *wrong* shape, then it dwindles, crumbles, is a husk, and the Brollachan sloughs it as a snake its skin and takes another. We came in time with Susan: had we not, she would have withered like the white lily in the black frost. Now she is safe: if we can find her.'

'But are you sure it's Sue upstairs?' said Colin. 'When I touched her hand last night it felt – different – not a hand at all.'

'Do not worry,' said Cadellin. 'That would be a memory from an earlier shape: such things linger with the Brollachan: its mind is slow to change. Do not men who have lost a limb often feel pain in hand or foot that is not there?'

'But wheer's all this getting us?' said Gowther. 'Susan's lying up theer, and we conner wake her. Summat'll have to be done.'

The wizard sighed. 'I do not know the answer, farmer Mossock. The Brollachan drove her from her body, and where she is now I cannot see. She is beyond my magic: we shall call on other powers to find her, and until she is found she must lie here, and the bracelet of Angharad Goldenhand must never leave her wrist.'

'I wish it never had,' said Albanac. 'I brought it to her the moment Atlendor gave it back to me, but that was not soon enough.'

'Now see here,' said Gowther, 'how long is this caper

to go on for?'

'It will not be a short business,' said the wizard. 'Weeks – months – let us hope not years. She is far away.'

'Then it's the doctor for her, reet here and now,' said Gowther. 'I've had enough messing about.'

'Farmer Mossock, you would pour water on burning oil!' cried the wizard. 'Is it not clear to you yet? This is no matter for mortal skills. What would happen? She would be taken from us. Our task would grow five-fold.'

'Ay, but hospital's the place for her if she's going to stay like this: she'll need special feeding, for one thing.'

'No. We shall take care of her. She will be safe with us. Farmer Mossock, the worst you could do is what you plan to do. Susan's danger, *our* danger, will increase if you do not go our way in this.'

Gowther looked searchingly at the wizard. 'Well — I dunner like this at all – but I've seen enough of you to tell that you know what's what in these goings on. So we'll compromise. I may as well be hung for a sheep as a lamb. Unless Susan takes a turn for the worse, I'll do nowt about it for the next three days.'

'Three days!' said Cadellin. 'There is little can be done in three days.'

'Ay, well, I wouldner know,' said Gowther. 'But that's the way it is.'

'Then we must accept it, and hope for second thoughts.' The wizard rose from his chair. 'Colin, will you be at Goldenstone at noon tomorrow? There is something that Susan will need.'

Colin turned off the road on to the track that ran along the wood side. On his left were pine and oak, on his right the fields and hills.

He came to the grey block of sandstone that stood at

the border of the path and was called the Goldenstone. It was so crudely shaped that few people would notice that it carried the mark of tools, and was not one of the many outcrops on the Edge, but had been placed there at some time of the world for a forgotten purpose. Uthecar and Albanac were sitting with their backs against it.

'Sit you here, Colin,' said Albanac. 'It is as dry as anywhere. How is Susan?'

'She's no different. Have you found anything that'll help?'

'We have not,' said Uthecar. 'Though rest has been far from our heads and sleep from our eyes since we left you.'

'Cadellin uses all his power,' said Albanac, 'but not even he can see where she is. But take good heart to you: we shall not give up, and others help us. We have come now from Redesmere: the Lady of the Lake sends you this – there will be no need of other food.' He handed Colin a leather bottle. 'Wine from the table of Angharad Goldenhand has many virtues.'

'Thank you,' said Colin. 'But you are going to find Sue, aren't you? It is just a question of time? And in what sort of a place is she? How can she be somewhere else when she's lying in bed?'

'I will not lie to you,' said Albanac. 'The Susan that sleeps is Length and Breadth and Height: but the real Susan is none of this. The two you have always known as one, but the Brollachan split them like a new-whetted blade in kindling.'

'I am thinking,' said Uthecar, 'I am thinking that Cadellin will not find her.'

'He must, and will,' said Albanac. 'I had not thought to see you so quickly cowed.'

'Nay, you take me wrong. I am thinking that the High Magic is too keen for the task.'

'I do not understand.'

'You try too hard. Be not so nimble-witted!' said Uthecar. 'Consider: it is said that the sword that lies by the Sleeper in Fundindelve would cleave a hair on water, draw blood from the wind. But would you use its temper to fell this oak? So here: the Brollachan is of the Old Evil — it does not move on such airy planes as Cadellin knows. For the Old Evil the Old Magic is best. Against an army a thousand strong give me the king's sword, but for this oak I would be having the cottar's axe.'

'I had not thought that way,' said Albanac. 'You may be right. And we must leave no hope untried. But what Old Magic is there now? It sleeps, and should not be woken.'

'Alas, I have no head for such things,' said Uthecar. 'I was asking the lios-alfar, but they would never look so low.'

'But what shall we do?' cried Albanac. Uthecar's words seemed to have put new life into him. Even Colin, though bewildered, caught some of the fire.

'If I were thinking, not knowing much of lore, of what would be the strongest charm for all ill times,' said Uthecar, 'I should say the Mothan. But where it may grow in this flat southern land, I could not be telling.'

'The Mothan!' said Albanac. 'I have heard of it! But it is a magic plant, not easy to be found, and we have three days.'

'Tell me about it,' said Colin. 'I'll find it.'

Uthecar looked at him. 'Ay. It would take such purpose as I see in you.

'It is a fickle plant: it grows only on the heights of the old, straight track, and flowers only in the full of the moon.'

'It's full moon tomorrow night!' cried Colin. 'Where is this track?'

Both he and Albanac were on their feet, but Uthecar stayed where he was.

'There are many tracks. All are lost. I know of two beyond Minith Bannawg, but not even an elf could be there in time. There may be others here. If you stand on the old, straight track when the full moon will rise along it, then you will see it: it is hidden at all other times.'

'Are there any here?' said Colin wildly, turning to Albanac.

'I do not know. Again, I have heard of them: but they were made at a time before dwarfs, and before wizards. And they are part of the Old Magic, though we do not know their purpose, and dead things stir when *it* moves.'

'Look! I've *got* to find this track! There must be a way. Why did you tell me about it if you knew it was no use?'

'I was wondering if the track is known here,' said Uthecar. 'Alas, it is not. But catch courage! It is the Old Magic, simple, warm. Faith and resolution can touch its heart. If the Mothan is to be found, you will find it, though I know not where it may be.'

'But how shall I start to look for it?' said Colin.

'Believe that help will come: search: try: think of Susan: never lose heart. Be here tomorrow at this time, and we may have better news.'

Colin walked back to Highmost Redmanhey unaware of his surroundings. The old, straight track: the old, straight track. It was all so vague. The old, straight track. Yet he knew that somewhere he had heard of it before Uthecar had mentioned it, which was ridiculous, since how could he know about something magical that was little more than hearsay to those who lived with magic? But the harder he tried, the further memory receded, and the more certain he became that he could answer the question if he could remember.

Back at the farm Colin ate a dismal meal. He had given up the search for the old, straight track, and was preoccupied with thoughts of Susan. The Mossocks ate in silence, their faces drawn with worry.

Then, as often happens when the mind has left a problem, the picture that had been eluding him rose through Colin's thoughts.

'*Got it!*'

He leapt from his chair and raced upstairs to his room. He dived across the bed, and hauled Gowther's suède-covered ledger from its shelf. Somewhere in these four hundred and fifty pages was a reference to the old, straight track: he knew he had seen it: now the entry stood out in his mind: it was opposite a page of heraldic notes: there was a drawing of a coat of arms—a chevron between three boars' heads. But even so, Colin was in such a state that he had to thumb through the book twice before he found it, and then, as he read, the dry scholarship of the rector's notes seemed so removed from the excitement of magic that he began to doubt.

'Today I walked the line of an old, straight track-way, made by our rude forbears, I am forced to believe, prior to the coming of the antique Roman to these shores.

I have followed this road from Mobberley to the Edge. It was engineered, if that be the term, at so remote an era that all record of it is lost, save the frequent mounds and stones erected to indicate the way. Of these, the Beacon and the Goldenstone are the most remarkable on the Edge, and from the latter, where I terminated my excursion, it seemed that the trackway was aligned with the peak of Shining Tor, which stands distant nine miles towards Buxton.

One cannot cease to marvel at the felicity of these unknown architects, who, ignorant of all the arts of science —'

Colin shut the book. The elation had gone. But what else

was there to hang on to except this? He had to try.

'Are you all reet, lad?' said Bess when he went downstairs. 'You look as if you've lost a shilling and found sixpence.'

'No: it's all right,' said Colin. 'I'm sorry about that. It was something I'd remembered in the old book. Do you know where the Beacon is on the Edge?'

'Ay,' said Gowther. 'It's the highest part of the Edge. You know when you go along the top path from Castle Rock to Stormy Point? Well, just before you bear left, it's the round hill above you on your right. You conner miss it: theer used to be a stone hut on the top, and you con still see the foundations.'

'Do you mind if I go and look at it this afternoon?' said Colin.

'Nay, of course not,' said Bess. 'It'll give you summat to do, and theer's nowt like being active to take your mind off things.'

'Thanks; I shan't be long.'

Gowther was right. There was no mistaking the Beacon. It was a smooth-skinned mound, obviously artificial, and it stood clear of the trees on the highest point of the Edge. It looked like a tumulus.

Colin walked all over and about the mound, but the only track was modern, and anything but straight.

From the Beacon, Colin set off through the trees to the Goldenstone, which was a quarter of a mile away, along no track that he could see. On reaching it, Colin continued in a straight line past the stone, over a slight rise of ground, until he came to the edge of the wood, a few yards further on. From here, across the fields, was the high ridge of the Pennines, and at one point, directly ahead of Colin, the line of hills rose to a shallow but definite peak. Again, nowhere was there any hint of a track.

Shining Tor, presumably, thought Colin. Well, the notes were right, at least. I suppose I'd better tell Albanac. It's all there is to go on, unless *he's* turned something up.

CHAPTER 8

Shining Tor

'It could be,' said Albanac. 'It could be. Though we think of Goldenstone as elvish, I remember it is said the elves found it here when the road was made.'

' "Could be"!' shouted Uthecar. 'You would doubt the wolf has teeth unless they were tearing the throat of you! "Could be"! It *is*! It *is*! The Old Magic has quickened to our need: it has shown you the way to its heart, the old, straight track from the Beacon hill. There you must stand this night, Colin, and take what chance may come.'

'That is what I do not like,' said Albanac. 'Strange memories linger on the Beacon.'

'What of that? I shall be there, Colin, and my sword shall keep you.'

For Colin the rest of the day dragged heavily. He checked in his diary and in the newspapers the time when the moon should rise: then he was struck by an agony of thought. What if it should be a cloudy night? Would that make a difference? So he read the weather forecasts and climbed the Riddings three times to look at the sky. But he need not have feared. It was a clear night when at last he crept from the farm-house and made his way to the wood.

He met Uthecar at the Goldenstone, and they walked together through the quiet darkness.

'Will the moon rise along the track?' said Colin.

'That is our greatest chance,' said Uthecar. 'But I think it will. If it does not, then there is little we can do.'

'And how shall I know the Mothan when I see it?'

'It grows alone among the rocks: there are five points to its leaves, its roots are red, and it mirrors the moon. You will know it when you see it.'

They climbed up the mound on which the Beacon had stood. At the top was a little sandy space, and a few blocks of sandstone. They settled themselves upon the blocks, and waited. The dwarf's sword lay across his knees.

'What am I to do with the Mothan when I find it?' said Colin.

'Take the flower, and a few of the leaves,' said Uthecar, 'and give them to Susan: but see to it that you harm not the root, nor take all the leaves.'

They sat quietly. Colin did not want to speak. He could not keep his voice from trembling, and all the time he was short of breath. Then, after repeatedly looking at his watch, Colin stood up and began to pace backwards and forwards across the top of the mound. He peered at the darkness. Nothing moved or showed. At last he sank down upon a stone and put his head between his hands.

'It's no good,' he said flatly. 'The moon should have risen five minutes ago.'

'Do not grieve yet,' said Uthecar. 'The moon will have to climb from behind the hills. Stand up, Colin: be ready.'

The dwarf moved down a little way from Colin, leaving him alone at the top of the mound. There was a moment of silence, then Colin said:

'Listen. Can you hear that?'

'I hear night-sound: that is all.'

'Listen! It's music – like voices calling, and bells of ice! *And look! There's the track!*'

Suddenly through the trees and over the Beacon hill a shimmering line had flowed, a mesh of silver threads, each glistening, alive. Colin had seen something like it once before, on a rare morning when the sun had cut a

path through the dewed, invisible carpet of spiders'
webs that covered the fields. That had been nothing to
the beauty he saw now. The track quivered under his
feet, and he gazed at it as though spellbound.

'Run!' called Uthecar. 'Do not waste your time!'

'But which way?' cried Colin. 'It stretches left and
right as far as I can see!'

'To the east! To the hills! Quickly! The track will be
lost when the moon passes from it! Run! Run! And
fortune follow you!'

Colin leaped down the hill, and his feet were winged
with silver. Trees blurred around him, once he felt Goldenstone hard beneath him, then he burst from the wood,
and there was the old, straight track, dipping and flow-
ing over the rounded fields and rising, a silver thread like
a distant mountain stream, up the face of the hills to the
peak of Shining Tor, and behind it the broad disc of the
moon, white as an elvan shield.

On, on, on, on, faster, faster the track drew him,
flowed through him, filled his lungs and his heart and his
mind with fire, sparked from his eyes, streamed from his
hair, and the bells and the music and the voices were all
of him, and the Old Magic sang to him from the depths
of the earth and the caverns of the night-blue sky.

Then the track rose before him, and he was in the
hills. The moon was clear above Shining Tor. And as he
sprang up the wall of the high cliff peak the path faded
like a veil of smoke. Weight took his body and pulled
him from the hill, but Colin cried one great cry and
snatched for the cliff top: the bells were lost in the sobbing of his breath, the drumming of his blood.

He opened his eyes: rough gritstone lay against his
cheek, grey in the moon. From between his fingers, clut-
ching the rock, curled leaves, five-pointed, and beneath
the hollow of his hand was a faint gleam of moonlight.

Over Wildboarclough the cone of Shuttlingslow stood apart from the long ridges, watchtower to the plain which lay like a sea from Rivington Pike to the surge of Moel Fammaw. But Colin saw none of it, for his eyes and his being were fixed on the delicate Mothan which he held cupped in his hands.

He had taken the flower and two of the leaves. The petals flickered with a cold, glow-worm light, and the fine hairs on the leaves were silver. Minutes passed: then Colin folded the Mothan gently into a leather bag that Uthecar had given him for the purpose, and looked about him.

The old, straight track had vanished, but below Shining Tor the road from Buxton began its winding drop into Macclesfield. Colin walked along the ridge to the end of the cliff, and picked his way over the rough moorland down to the road.

It was midnight. The road was strange, cold, smooth under his feet after the reed-clumps and boulders of Shining Tor. Once the flush of excitement had passed, and it had passed quickly with the climb from the hill, he felt tired – and increasingly ill at ease. The night was so still, and the road so lonely in the moonlight. But then Colin thought of Susan lying in bed at Highmost Redmanhey, and of the Mothan in his pocket, and of the wonder of the evening, and his steps grew lighter.

Light steps. That was what he could hear: behind him. He stopped and listened. Nothing. Looked. The road was empty. It must be an echo, thought Colin, and he set off again. But now he was listening consciously, and soon he began to sweat.

He heard his footsteps hard on the road, and after them an echo from the drystone wall and the hill, and through footstep and echo a pad, pad of feet, and, by the sound, the feet were bare.

He stopped. Nothing. Looked. The road was empty.

But the moon threw shadows.

Colin set his teeth, and walked faster. Footstep. Echo. Footstep. Echo. Footstep. Echo. *Footstep. Echo.* He breathed again. Nerves! Nothing but – pad, pad, pad. Colin spun round. Did any shadow move?

'Who's there?' he shouted.

'Air! Air! Air!' said the hill.

'I – I can see you, you know!'

'Ho! Ho! Ho!'

It says much for Colin that he did not run. The panic was close, but he thrust it down and forced his brain to reason. How far to Macclesfield? Four miles? No point in running, then. He slowly turned, and began to walk. And although he could not go ten paces without looking back, he drew steadily away from Shining Tor. He saw nothing. But the footsteps that were never quite echoes stayed with him.

After half an hour Colin was beginning to think that he would perhaps reach the town, for whatever was following him seemed content to follow: it never shortened the distance between them. Then, approaching a sharp corner, Colin heard something that stopped him dead. It was a new sound, and it came from in front: hoofs – the sound of a horse walking slowly.

He looked behind him. Still nothing. But he could not go back. And away from the road there was too much unknown. Yet why should he be afraid of this new sound? Colin was at such a pitch that he was afraid of his own voice. He could make no decision: he was caught.

His eyes were fixed on the road where it licked out of sight like a black tongue. The gentle clop of the hoofs seemed to go on for ever. The road would always be empty —

It was a black horse, and its rider was cloaked and wore a wide-brimmed hat.

'Albanac!'

Colin staggered forward, laughing. A touch of reality – even such reality – and the scene had changed. Colin saw himself in perspective. It was a fine night of full moon among peaceful hills, and Susan was waiting for him to bring the Mothan. From the time he had left the Beacon till now he had been on another plane of existence: it had been too much for his imagination.

'Albanac!'

'Colin! I thought you would be somewhere on the road. Have you the Mothan?'

'Yes!'

'Come, then. We'll be away to Susan.'

Albanac reached down and lifted Colin into the saddle before him, and turned the horse towards Macclesfield.

'Why, Colin, you are wet and trembling. Is anything amiss?'

'No. It's just that it's all been a bit unsettling. I've had quite a time!'

'Ay, so I see.'

As he said this, the horse turned its head and looked back along the road. It snorted, and its ears flattened to its skull.

Albanac twisted in the saddle. Colin, half enfolded in the cloak, could not see the road behind, but he felt Albanac's body stiffen, and heard the breath hiss through his teeth. Then the reins slapped the high neck, and the horse leapt away with all the tempest of its fairy blood, and the speed of its going drove questions back into Colin's throat, and the night filled his ears, and the cloak cracked in the wind.

Nor did Albanac stop until they came to the Riddings, and they looked down upon Highmost Redmanhey, timber and plaster magpied by the moon, and a lamp in the window of the room where Susan lay.

'Why is there a light?' said Colin.

'All is well,' said Albanac. 'Cadellin waits for us.'

The little room was crowded. When Colin opened the door Bess cried, 'Oh, wheer have you been? You shouldner have —'

'That'll do, lass,' said Gowther gently. 'Did you get what you went for, Colin?'

'Yes.'

'And are you all reet?'

'Yes.'

'Well that's all as matters. Let's see what's to be done, then.'

Colin took the flower and leaves from his pouch.

'You have run well,' said Uthecar. 'It is the Mothan. Give it to your sister.'

'Here you are,' said Colin, and handed the Mothan to Cadellin. But the wizard shook his head.

'No, Colin. This is the Old Magic: it will not bend to my mind. Let Uthecar take it: he is better skilled in this lore.'

'Nay, Cadellin Silverbrow,' said the dwarf. 'It will not hear me. Mine is not the need. It is through Colin that it moves. Do you fold the flower within the leaves and put them in her mouth.'

Colin went to the bed. He folded the Mothan tightly and opened Susan's jaws with his finger just enough to work the pellet past her teeth. Then he stood back, and for everyone the silence was like a band of steel about the head. Three minutes went by: nothing happened.

'This is daft,' said Bess.

'Quiet!' said Uthecar hoarsely.

Another long silence. Colin thought he was going to collapse. His legs were trembling with the effort of concentration.

'Listen!' said Albanac.

Far away, and, if anywhere, above them, they heard a faint baying, and the deep winding of a horn. The baying grew nearer, and now there was the jingling of harness. The horn sounded again: it was just outside the window. And Susan opened her eyes.

She stared wildly about her, as though she had been woken in the middle of a dream. Then she sat up, and pulled a face, and put her hand to her mouth. But Uthecar sprang across the room and hit Susan hard between the shoulder blades with the flat of his hand.

'Swallow it!'

Susan could not help herself. She hiccupped under the blow, and the Mothan was gone. Then Susan leapt out of bed. She ran to the window and threw it open so recklessly that the lamp was knocked into the yard below and exploded in a glare of paraffin. Susan leant out of the window, and Colin blundered across the darkened room and grabbed her by the shoulders, for she seemed intent on something that made her forget danger.

'Celemon!' she cried. 'Celemon! Stay for me!'

Colin pulled her back over the sill – then clutched the frame to save himself from falling, for the shock of what he saw in the sky above the farm took his legs from under him.

He could not say if they were stars, or what they were. The sky was a haze of moonlight, and in the haze it seemed as though the stars had formed new constellations, constellations that moved, had life, and took the shape and spangled outline of nine young women on horseback, gigantic, filling the heavens. They milled round above the farm, hawks on hand, and among them pranced hounds with glittering eyes and jewelled collars. The riders wore short tunics, and their hair gleamed along the sky. Then the horn sounded again, the horses reared and flared over the plain, and the night poured shooting-stars into the western sea.

Only Colin had seen this. As he turned back to the room Bess appeared in the doorway with a lamp. Susan stood facing the window, tears on her cheek. But when light filled the room she relaxed, and sighed.

'How is it with you, Susan?' said Cadellin.

She looked at him. 'Cadellin. Bess. Gowther. Uthecar. Colin. Albanac. Oh! Then what was that? I'd forgotten you.'

'Sit on the bed,' said Cadellin. 'Tell us what you know of these past days. But first, Mistress Mossock, will you bring Susan food and drink? It is all she needs to secure her now.'

This was soon done, and while she ate, Susan told her story. She spoke hesitantly, as though trying to describe something to herself as much as to anyone else.

'I remember falling into water,' she said, 'and everything went black: I held my breath until the pain made me let go, but just then the water rushed away from me in the dark, and – well – although the darkness was the same, I was somewhere else, floating – nowhere in particular, just backwards and forwards, and round in nothing. You know how when you're in bed at night you can imagine the bed's tilted sideways, or the room's sliding about? It was like that.

'That wasn't too bad, but I didn't like the noises. There were squeakings and gratings going on all round me – voices – no, not quite voices; they were just confused sounds; but they came from throats. Some were near and others far away. This went on for a long time, and I didn't like it. But I wasn't frightened or worried about what was going to happen to me – though I'm frightened now when I think of it! I didn't like being where I was, but at the same time I couldn't think of anywhere else that I wanted to be. And then all at once I felt a hand catch hold of my wrist and pull me upwards. There was a light, and I heard someone shouting – I think now it was Albanac – and I started to move faster than ever; so fast that I was dizzy, and the light got brighter and brighter, and it made no difference when I shut my eyes. Then I began to slow down, and the glare didn't hurt so much, and I could see the outline of the hand that was holding me. And then I seemed to break through a skin of light, and I was lying in shallow water at the edge of a sea, and standing over me was a woman, dressed in red and white, and we were holding each other's wrist and our bracelets were linked together – and Cadellin! I've just realised! Hers was the same as mine – the one Angharad gave me!'

'Ay, it would be,' said the wizard quietly. 'No matter: go on.'

'Well, she undid her bracelet and slipped it out of mine, and we walked along the beach, and she said her name was Celemon and we were going to Caer Rigor. I didn't feel there was any need to ask questions: I accepted everything as it came, like you do in a dream.

'We joined the others who were waiting for us on a rocky headland, and we rode out above the sea towards Caer Rigor, and everyone was excited and talked of home. Then suddenly there was this bitter taste in my mouth and all the others had it, too, and no matter how hard we rode, we couldn't move forward. Celemon said we must turn back, so we did, and then I felt dizzy again, and the taste in my mouth got worse until I thought I was going to be sick, and I couldn't keep my balance, and I fell from the horse, over and over into the sea, or fog, or whatever it was. I was falling for hours, and then I hit something hard. I'd closed my eyes to stop myself from being sick, and when I opened them I was here.

'But where is Celemon? Shan't I see her again?'

'I do not doubt it,' said the wizard. 'Some day you will meet, and ride over the sea to Caer Rigor, and there will be no bitterness to draw you back. But everything in its time. And now you must rest.'

They left Susan with Bess and went downstairs to the kitchen.

Colin was light-headed with exhaustion and bewilderment, and on the way downstairs his attempt to describe what he had seen when he had pulled Susan from the window was lost on all but Cadellin, who seemed to take it all as confirmation of his own thoughts.

'Caer Rigor,' said the wizard. 'Caer Rigor. Oh, we are in deep water now. Caer Rigor. It is well you found the Mothan when you did, Colin, for once there, neither the High nor the Old Magic would have brought her back.

Three times the fulness of Prydwen we went into it:
Except seven, none returned from Caer Rigor.

'That is how it is remembered in song. Ay, it is not often the Old Magic does so much good.'

'What do you mean?' said Colin. 'It's not Black Magic, is it? Please explain! And what happened to Sue?'

'It is difficult,' said the wizard. 'I would rather leave it till we have rested. But if you are bent on this, then I must tell you – though at the end you may understand less than you do now.

'No, Colin, the Old Magic is not evil: but it has a will of its own. It may work to your need, but not to your command. And again, there are memories about the Old Magic that wake when it moves. They, too, are not evil of themselves, but they are fickle, and wrong for these times.'

'It is indeed so,' said Albanac. 'The Hunter was on the road.'

'You saw him?' said Cadellin sharply.

'I saw him. He came down with Colin from his bed on Shining Tor. He would want to know who had roused him.'

'What?' said Colin. 'Who's this? On the road? I heard

someone following me, or I thought I did, but when I met you it all seemed so silly.'

'Ay, well perhaps it was.'

'Yes, but what are you talking about?'

'An old memory,' said the wizard. 'No harm came of it, so no more need be said now. Let me try to explain what Susan has just told us. That is what may affect us all.'

'Surely to goodness you dunner reckon much on that!' said Gowther. 'It was nobbut a dream! She said so herself.'

'She said it was *like* a dream,' said Cadellin. 'I wish I could dismiss it so: but it is truth, and I suspect there is even more than she remembers.

'The Brollachan thrust her from the one level of the world that men are born to, down into the darkness and unformed life that is called Abred by wizards. From there she was lifted to the Threshold of the Summer Stars, as far beyond this world of yours as Abred is below: and few have ever gone so far, fewer still returned, and none at all unchanged.

'She has ridden with the Shining Ones, the Daughters of the Moon, and they came with her from behind the north wind. Now she is here. But the Shining Ones did not leave Susan of choice, for through her they may wake their power in the world – the Old Magic, which has long been gone from here. It is a magic beyond our guidance: it is magic of the heart, not of the head: it can be felt, but not known: and in that I see no good.

'And Susan was not prey of the Brollachan by chance. Vengeance was there, too.

'She was saved, and is protected, only by the Mark of Fohla – her blessing and her curse. For it guards her against the evil that would crush her, and it leads her ever further from the ways of human life. The more she wears it, the more need there is to do so. And it is too late now to take it off.

'Is that not enough, without calling the Old Magic from its sleep? I should be lighter in my heart if I knew that what you have quickened this night could as easily be laid to rest.'

Colin lay awake, the day and night racing through his head, long after the wizard had gone. So much was un-answered, so much not understood, so much had been achieved – in spite of himself, he felt : he had been only a tool. But Susan was safe, Susan was – Colin sat up in bed. Beneath the open window he had heard a soft, familiar sound. Pad, pad, pad, pad, pad. He jumped out of bed and crept to the window.

The farm-house hid the yard in shadow. Colin listened, but there was now no sound. He peered – and could not choke the cry that leapt in his throat. The roof's shadow was a straight line along the bottom of the shippon wall across the yard, and above this line was the shadow of a pair of antlers, the curved, proud antlers of a stag.

At the noise the shadow moved and was lost. Pad, pad, pad. The night was silent once the footsteps had died away.

CHAPTER 9

The Horsemen of Donn

The next morning Susan appeared to be in no way the worse for all that had happened to her. She looked well and felt well. But Bess insisted on her staying in bed, and the doctor was called. She was quite put out when the doctor said he could find nothing wrong with Susan.

Days passed. The children spent most of the time discussing what each of them had seen and done. Susan found that she was rapidly forgetting what had happened to her between the fall into the quarry and her swallowing of the Mothan. It *was* like a dream; clear and more real than anything else at first, but soon lost under the more tangible flood of waking impressions. She could add little to the brief tale she had told within minutes of her return.

She was more concerned over Colin's experiences with the Brollachan, and though he gave her only an outline of what had happened, his story broke her sleep for several nights.

Colin went into more detail when trying to describe what he had seen in the sky after he had pulled Susan from the window, but he found it beyond him. The clearest picture he could give was to liken the riders and their hounds to the figures in the star-maps in an old encyclopedia at home, where the stars of the constellations formed part of the outline drawn by an artist to show that the kite of Orion was really three-quarters of a giant, and the W of Cassiopeia was a woman sitting in a chair. But none of this matched Susan's knowledge of the riders. To her, Celemon had been a normal person, as solid in her state of existence then as Colin was to her now. She could not grasp the rest.

And neither of them could make anything of the footsteps Colin had heard, nor did Gowther help when they asked him if there were any deer on the Edge.

'Why, no,' he said. 'Theer used to be some at Alderley Park in Lord Stanley's time, but they went years ago.'

Yet what excited Susan more than anything else was Colin's finding of the old, straight track, and his journey along it to the Mothan. And when they climbed up from the Holywell late one day, and saw the Beacon mound dark in starlight above them, Susan could not pass it by.

They had been to Fundindelve at the request of Albanac to find out what Atlendor had been able to do with Susan's bracelet. It was a short answer: he had done nothing: the power was not his. Their visit had dragged into a prolonged argument about whether Susan should go north with Atlendor, and always the talk had kept swinging round from the elves to the Brollachan, both being at the front of Albanac's worries.

'For,' he had said, 'I do not like to leave, and the Brollachan still loose. It is well away, but we must find it, and just now there is no finger of a road to its hiding-place. Yet soon the lios-alfar must ride, and I am pledged to ride with him. That is not a choice I am wanting to make.'

It had been a tiring and inconclusive discussion. But now there was the Beacon.

'Let's go up,' said Susan.

'All right,' said Colin. 'There's not much to look at, though.'

'I know. But I'd like to watch the moon rise – I suppose there's no chance of seeing the track, but I want to be there, so that I'll know how you felt; if that doesn't sound silly.'

'Wait a minute,' said Colin. 'What about Bess and Gowther? It's late already, and it'll be another half-hour,

I'd say, before the moon rises.'

'They know where we are,' said Susan over her shoulder. 'And I don't think Gowther'll be bothered. Come on!'

Colin followed Susan up the bare slope of the Beacon, and they sat on the stone blocks at the top. He pointed out the line of the track as accurately as he could remember it. Then it was a matter of waiting for the moon, and before long the children were both bored and cold.

'Have you got a match with you?' said Susan.

'No, I don't think so.'

'Well, have a look.'

Colin turned out his pockets, and at the bottom of the fluff, crumbs, and balls of silver paper he found one grubby matchstick.

'Do you think it's safe to light a fire,' said Colin.

'It should be. There aren't any trees here, and this sand will stop it from spreading.'

The children gathered kindling of rowan twigs, and among the trees at the bottom of the hill they found a naked, long-fallen pine, as smooth as bone.

'Don't build it too dense,' said Susan, 'or it won't start.'

From match to twig to branch the light grew, until the pine wood spurted fire. The flames leapt high, and within seconds the whole pile roared. Colin and Susan threw the wood they had gathered on to the flames, but the more they threw, the faster the wood burnt.

'Steady,' said Colin. 'It'll get out of control if we don't watch it. There's too much resin in the wood.'

But Susan was carried away by the urgency of the fire. She ran down to the pine tree, and began to pull on a heavier branch.

'Here, come and give me a hand, Colin! This'll make it really go!'

'No!' Colin's voice was suddenly tense. 'Don't put any more on. There's something wrong. I'm cold.'

'It's only the wind,' said Susan. 'Oh, do hurry! There'll be nothing left!'

She swung all her weight on the branch, and stumbled as it broke from the trunk. Then she started to drag the branch backwards up the hill. Colin ran to her, and caught hold of her arm.

'Sue! Can't you feel it? It's not giving out any heat!'

'Who now brings fire to the mound at the Eve of Gomrath?' said a cold, thin voice behind them.

Colin and Susan turned.

The flames were a scarlet curtain between hill and sky, and within them, and a part of them, were three men. At first their tall shapes and haggard faces danced and merged with the blazing pine branches, and were as unstable as any picture that the mind sees in the shadows of a fire: but even while the children looked, they became more solid, rounded, and independent of the flames through which they stared. Then they were real, and terrible.

They were dressed all in red: red were their tunics, and red their cloaks; red their eyes, and red their long manes of hair bound back with circlets of red gold; three red shields on their backs, and three red spears in their hands; three red horses under them, and red was the harness. Red were they all, weapons and clothing and hair, both horses and men.

'Who – who are you?' whispered Colin. 'What do you want?'

The middle horseman stood in his saddle, and raised a glowing spear above his head.

'Lo, my son, great the news! Wakeful are the steeds we ride, the steeds from the ancient mound. Wakeful are we, the Horsemen of Donn, Einheriar of the Herlathing. Lo, my son!'

'I ride! I ride!'

A lone figure came from the trees. His face was stern, heavy-browed, his beard plaited, two-forked, his mane black, awful, majestic. He wore a tunic of coarse hair without any cloak, and a round shield with five gold circles on it, and rivets of white bronze, hung from his neck. In his hand was an iron flail, having seven chains, triple-twisted, three-edged, with seven spiked knobs at the end of every chain. His horse was black, and golden-maned.

Now down they rode, the red and the white and the wild king, over Monks' Heath, a mile to the loneliness of Sodger's Hump – the Soldier's Hump – with its ring of pines, where strange, pale lights are said to move among the trees on certain nights of winter. But now the light was one and red.

'Wakeful is Fallowman son of Melimbor! Wakeful is Bagda son of Toll! Ride, Einheriar of the Herlathing!'

'We ride! We ride!'

Round heads of black hair they had, the same length at neck and brow, and their eyes gleamed darkness. They wore long-hooded, black cowls, and carried black, wide-grooved swords, well balanced for the stroke. The horses were black, even to the tongues.

Wood and valley and stream swept by, field and hedge and lane, by Capesthorne and Whisterfield, three miles and more, Windyharbour, Withington, Welltrough, and there stood Broad hill, the Tunsted of old, and its pines flared red under the spear.

'Wakeful are the sons of Ormar! Wakeful Maedoc, Midhir, Mathramil! Ride, Einheriar of the Herlathing!'

'We ride! We ride!'

Their cloaks were blue as rain-washed sky, their yellow manes spread wide upon their shoulders: five-barbed javelins in their hands, and their silver shields with fifty knobs of burnt gold on each, and the bosses of precious stones. They shone in the night as if they were the sun's rays. The horses' hoofs were polished brass and their hides like cloth of gold.

Now the Einheriar were complete. They turned towards Alderley and the Beacon hill, and for a long time after the tracks of the horses endured in the turf and on the rocks with the fury of the riding, and the air behind them was all aglow with little sparks.

CHAPTER 10

Lord of the Herlathing

Colin thought he was going to die. Cool waves rolled over him, shutting him off from the singing pain in his head and the one bruise of body. He could no longer cry out against the pain, for his nerves and muscles seemed to have been shaken out of all co-ordination, and he gasped as silently as a fish.

For Susan the ride to the Beacon was less hard, but her mind was dazed by the pace and shock, until the finger of the burning shone through the trees.

The riders approached the Beacon without any slackening of speed, and when they reached it they swung in a circle about the mound, and pulled their horses to a skidding halt. The leader rose slowly to the top of the mound and into the fire. He stretched his spear downwards and touched the ground with its point, and Susan had her wish. The old, straight track flowed from the spear like a band of molten steel from a furnace. But now it was not moon-silvered, as Colin had seen it, but a tumbling river of red flame-curls which darted through the wood and beyond sight.

The horseman lifted both his arms and threw back his head :

Wakeful is He in the Hill of the Dawn!
Wakeful is He to the flame of the Goloring!
From heat of the sun, and cold of the moon,
Come, Garanhir! Gorlassar! Lord of the Herlathing!

All was quiet. No one moved. Then faintly, from a distance, there came a voice, clear, like a blend of trees and wind, rivers and starlight; nearer, nearer, chanting, wild:

And am I not he that is called Gorlassar?
Am I not a prince in darkness?
Garanhir, the torment of battle!

Where are my Reapers that sing of war
And a lance-darting trembling of slaughter;
Of the booming of shields in the cry of the sword,
The bite of the blue-headed spear in the flesh,
The thirst of the deep-drinking arrows of wrath,
And ravens red with the warring?

And away among the trees appeared the figure of a man. He came loping to the Beacon along the old, straight track, and the light played on the muscles of his body in rippling patterns of black and red. He was huge and powerful, yet with the grace of an animal; at least seven feet tall, and he ran effortlessly. His face was long and thin, his nose pointed, and nostrils flared; his eyes night-browed, up-sweeping, dark as rubies; his hair red curls; and among the curls grew the antlers of a stag.

The horseman answered him:

Swift the hoof, and free the wind!
Wakeful are we to the flame of the Goloring!
From heat of the sun, and cold of the moon,
Hail, Garanhir! Gorlassar! Lord of the Herlathing!

Then he backed slowly from the fire, and when the runner came to the circle and sprang in a stride to the top of the mound, all the horses knelt, and the riders lifted their arms in silence.

Susan looked at him and was not afraid. Her mind could not accept him, but something deeper could. She knew what made the horses kneel. Here was the heart of all wild things. Here were thunder, lightning, storm; the slow beat of tides and seasons, birth and death, the need to kill and the need to make. His eyes were on her, yet she could not be afraid.

He stood alone and still in the cold flames, and they flowed round him and took his shape, so that he was outlined in blood, and scarlet tongues streamed upwards from the points of his antlers. He seemed to draw the light of the fire to himself; it dwindled, and the flames sank as though they were being pulled down through his flesh, and he grew, not in size, but in power, until the only light was that of the moon, and he stood black against it.

Then he spoke. 'It is long since wendfire kindled the Goloring. What men had remembered the Eve of Gomrath?'

The two riders carrying the children moved forward.

Colin felt deep eyes sweep through him, and an exhilaration, breathless as fear, lifted the pain from his body.

'It is good to wake when the moon stands on the hill.'

Something close to laughter stirred in his voice, and he bent down and set Colin upright astride the horse's neck. Then he turned to Susan, and was about to speak, when the rider lifted Susan's arm and showed the Mark of Fohla white on her wrist. It glowed with more than reflected silver, and the black characters engraved on it trembled as though they had life.

Lightly and briefly and without a word, the dark majesty dropped on one knee and Susan's hand was taken and laid upon a cold brow. Then he rose and lifted Colin and Susan from the horses, and put them down at the top of the mound, and turned away.

'Ride, Einheriar of the Herlathing!'

'We ride! We ride!'

Turf spattered the children, and for an instant the night was a tumult of rushing darkness, and then the children were alone.

They sank down on the stones, and looked at each other. 'That's – that's what I saw in the farmyard,' said Colin. 'That's what followed me.'

'They didn't care what happened to us,' said Susan blankly. 'They weren't interested in us at all.'

'He followed me right back to the farm.'

'But perhaps it's just as well,' said Susan: 'I wouldn't hope for much if they thought we were in the way.'

'Now was that bravely done?'

Colin and Susan jumped as the voice broke in on them. They peered in the direction from which it had come, and saw a dwarf standing under the trees.

'Uthecar!' shouted Colin, and they ran down the hill to meet him. 'Uthecar?'

'Who are you?' said Susan.

The dwarf looked at them. 'How shall we undo all this?' he said.

He was dressed in black, and there was a gold-hilted sword at his waist. His hair and beard were cleanly cut, and he carried himself proudly, and his voice was firm, so that the authority of his bearing removed all ill-nature from his words.

'I'm – sorry,' said Colin. 'What have we done wrong? Was all that our fault?'

'How was it not? None but fools would bring fire to the mound at any time; but to do so on this night of all nights of the year, and to burn wendwood! What is Cadellin thinking to let you from his sight? But come, we must see what your friends will do: it may not be too late to put them back in the mounds.'

'But we'll never find them!' cried Susan. 'They galloped off like the wind.'

'I think they have not gone far,' said the dwarf. 'Let us see.'

He stole away, and the children ran to keep up with him.

'But what's it all about?' said Colin. 'Who were they? And who was – he?'

'The Wild Hunt. The Herlathing. That is what you have sent out on us. It was enough to rouse the Hunter; he alone would have taken some laying. But now that the Einheriar ride after him we shall have to act quickly, or wide numbers will go to sleep with light in their eyes, and only the raven will find profit! But quiet now: I think we are on them.'

They had come to a cliff-top over a valley. The dwarf crawled to the edge and looked down. Colin and Susan joined him, but although they could hear movement at the foot of the cliff they could see nothing, for the rock overhung the ground below. They crawled along to where the cliff fell away to a sloping bank, and from this bank they could see clearly.

They were at the Holywell, and the second gate of Fundindelve. Along the path that ran past the well the Einheriar were drawn in line, and at the well, his antlers nearly level with the children's faces, was Garanhir, the Hunter. He held a cup of some white metal, and the riders took it one after the other and drank deeply, then lifted it and poured the last drops over their heads, and moved on.

For each rider Garanhir stooped and filled the cup from the well, and the water gleamed as the old, straight track had done at the touch of the spear, and all the marsh below shone red.

The dwarf worked back from the edge, and beckoned the children to follow him. He took them round the head of the valley and along the opposite ridge to where they could watch the silhouettes of the Einheriar against the dim glow.

'We are too late,' said the dwarf. 'Now that they have
drunk at the well this is wizard's work. Beard of the
Dagda! Are we to talk until all that ever slept is woken?
Which may happen yet, for once the Old Magic moves,
it moves deeply – even without the help of wendfires!

'Listen: do you see where we are now? Over the ridge
behind us are the iron gates; have you the opening of
them?'

'Yes – I think so,' said Susan.

'Then go to Cadellin: tell him that the Einheriar ride.
We shall keep watch here.'

'All right.'

Susan disappeared, and a few minutes later the ground
quivered under their feet, and the skyline of the ridge
was tinged with blue. Colin turned back to look at the
Holywell. Although the light was not good, he could tell
that the riders were milling together, and he could hear
hoofs stamping restlessly.

'I think they're going,' said Colin. 'What shall we do?'

A dry scrape of metal answered him. He glanced over
his shoulder, and saw the moon pale on the gold-hilted
sword as it came from its sheath, and pale in the eyes
behind the sword.

'We shall walk,' said the dwarf.

As she entered the tunnel, Susan thought she heard Colin
shout, but the noise of the rock and clang of the gates
drowned his voice, if it was his voice, and when the
echoes had died there was only silence thudding in her
ears. Susan hesitated: her hand reached out to the gates;
then she told herself that if anything had begun to
happen there was even more need to find Cadellin
quickly, so she turned and ran down the tunnel.

This was the long approach to the wizard's cave: the

whole labyrinth of Fundindelve lay between, and soon she realised that she did not know the way. In the tunnels her footsteps and breathing enclosed her in waves, but unnerving as this was, the blue-hazed infinity of the caverns was worse.

At last she was forced to rest, and while she leant, trembling, against a cave wall, her reason overcame her urgency, and from that moment she started to use her eyes. Even so, an hour had passed since she had left Colin before Susan found a tunnel that she knew, and it was another ten minutes before she reached the cave.

Uthecar and Albanac were with the wizard.

'What is it, Susan?' said Albanac, jumping to his feet.

'Einheriar! – Einheriar! – the Hunter!'

'The Einheriar?' said Cadellin. 'How do you know —?' He whirled round, and began to run up the short tunnel that led to the Holywell.

'Wait!' called Susan. 'They're just outside!'

The wizard took no notice of her, and after him raced Albanac, a stride ahead of Uthecar. By the time Susan reached the well they were all standing on the path, the dwarf studying the ground, and Cadellin looking out over the plain. The light had gone from the water, and the woods were silent. But then Uthecar said:

'They were here, and it was so.'

'And they have drunk of the well,' said Albanac.

'We must find them,' said Cadellin, 'though I doubt if they will be compelled to the mounds. It is bad.'

'It is worse,' said Uthecar. 'I am thinking that this is the Eve of Gomrath – and I smell wendfire.'

'It cannot be!' cried the wizard.

'I – I'm afraid we did it,' said Susan. 'We lit a fire on top of the Beacon. That's what started it all. They came out of the fire.'

'Why should you light a fire there?' said Cadellin in a voice that made Susan want to run.

'We were waiting for the moon to rise – and – we were – cold.'

The wizard shook his head. 'It is my fault,' he said to Albanac. 'I should have been stronger in my purpose. Come: we lose time. We must find their track.'

'Colin will know which way they went,' said Susan. 'They were keeping watch on here from across the valley.'

' "They"?' said the wizard.

'Yes,' said Susan. 'He and the dwarf: they're just this side of the iron gates.'

'What dwarf?' said Uthecar. 'There are no others here.'

'Yes there is,' said Susan. 'He's dressed in black, and —'

'Take us,' broke in Uthecar. 'And waste no breath.'

Susan felt a coldness in her heart. She set off along the path, and did not speak until she reached the spot where she had left Colin.

'Where are they?' She knew it was a useless question. 'What's happened?'

'Dressed in black, was he?' said Uthecar. 'And was there a golden hilt to his sword?'

'Yes: and his belt, and the straps below his knee were gold, too.'

'Do you know him?' said Cadellin.

'Know him? Ha! Know yon viper? I know him! But what has brought him south from Bannawg I will not guess, save that it is no good thing. For I tell you this: though you looked, you would not find from sea to sea a worse dwarf than Pelis the False.'

CHAPTER II

The Dale of Goyt

'There is a mind at work against these children,' said Cadellin. 'So much is certain.'

They had returned to the wizard's cave, and were sitting at the long table. Atlendor had joined them.

'But what can we do?' said Susan.

'Think, and hope,' said Cadellin.

'I would rather seek and find,' said Uthecar. 'Work your magic, Cadellin Silverbrow, but there may be more use of eyes and blades. Pelis is not here, and where he is, there I would be; for I am thinking the death of him is in my sword.'

'Then go,' said Cadellin. 'But take care in the night.'

The dwarf rose from the table, and was about to enter the tunnel when Atlendor spoke. 'Uthecar Hornskin, you will not go alone. It is on me to go with you.'

'As you wish,' said Uthecar shortly, and dwarf and elf left the cave together.

'Their swords will be about their own ears,' said Cadellin, 'if danger does not unite them.

'Now Susan, rest here. I must leave you for a while: but Albanac will stay.'

'But I couldn't!' said Susan. 'I must do something to find Colin.'

'If Atlendor and Uthecar cannot find him,' said the wizard, 'then you will not, and all that is left is magic.'

'I can't stay here and do nothing!'

'Susan! There is danger for you outside Fundindelve. You *must* stay here.'

'But Bess'll be nearly out of her mind!'

'I am glad you think of her,' said Cadellin. 'Do you see the pain you cause by meddling in our world? I must speak to farmer Mossock now and tell him that you will not go home until this matter is settled. I cannot hope that he will be persuaded, but you have left me no other choice.'

And though Susan argued, Cadellin remained firm, and both were angry when the wizard left the cave.

'I can't stay couped up here!' said Susan. 'I've got to get out and find Colin!'

Albanac passed his hand over his face. He looked exhausted.

'There is nothing we can do now, Susan. We may need all our strength later, so try to sleep. I know that I am spent.'

'But I've got to get out!'

'And how long is it since you were eating your heart away to get in?' said Albanac. 'If you cannot sleep, then sit here, and talk.'

Susan flung herself on to the bed of skins, and for some minutes was too choked with frustration to talk. But there were so many questions in her mind that this could not last.

'Albanac, who is the Hunter? And what did we do?'

'He is part of the Old Magic,' said Albanac. 'And though Cadellin may not agree, I think that what you did was not brought about by chance. The Old Magic has been woken, and it has moved in you, and I think it led you to the Beacon.

'In the time before the Old Magic was made to sleep, it was strongest on this night, the Eve of Gomrath, one of the four nights of the year when Time and Forever mingle. And wendfire was lit at the Goloring, which is now the Beacon, to bring the Einheriar from the mounds and the Hunter from Shining Tor. For the Old Magic is moon magic and sun magic, and it is blood magic, also, and there lie the Hunter's power and his need. He is from a cruel day of the world. Men have changed since they honoured him.'

'You keep saying the Old Magic has been woken,' said Susan, 'but if it's as strong as this, how did it ever come to die out?'

'That is the work of Cadellin,' said Albanac. 'To wizards, and their High Magic of thoughts and spells, the Old Magic was a hindrance, a power without shape or order: so they tried to destroy it. But it would not be destroyed: it would only sleep. And at this season called Gomrath, which lasts for seven nights, it sleeps but lightly.'

'So there's nothing bad about it at all,' said Susan. 'It just got in the way.'

'Yes. You may even say the wizards acted without right. But then, as ages pass, the world changes; so it is true that the Old Magic is wrong for these times. It does not fit the present scale of good and ill.'

'But it's more natural than all these spells,' said Susan. 'I think I understand it better than anything here.'

Albanac looked up. 'You would say that. For it is woman's magic, too, and the more I see, the more I know that the Mark of Fohla is part of it.'

'What does the Hunter do? What's he for?'

'Do? He *is*, Susan: that is enough. There you see the difference between the Old and the High. The High Magic was made with a reason; the Old Magic is a part of things. It is not *for* any purpose.'

Susan could feel the truth of what Albanac had said, although she could not understand it. She thought again of Colin. If only she had stopped when she heard him shout. Pelis the False.

'Albanac?'

'Mm?'

She rolled over to look. Albanac was sitting with his

head resting on his arms.

'Nothing; it's all right.'

Susan listened as Albanac's breathing grew deeper. He was asleep.

And there's nobody else here, she thought. That tunnel goes straight to the Holywell. What was it? Emalagra?

She moved quietly round the table, and tested every step until she reached the wall behind the well. She laid her hand on the long crack in the rock, and spoke the word of power.

The grinding of the rock echoed down the tunnel, and Susan forced herself through the opening as soon as it was wide enough to take her shoulder. Then she ran.

Uthecar and Atlendor sat in the moonlight on the wooden bench on Castle Rock, an outcrop that stood from the trees high above the plain.

'He is not in the wood,' said Uthecar. 'And from here the world is wide.'

'If he is not in the wood,' said Atlendor, 'think you he may be under it?'

'Is it that the lios-alfar have cunning?' said Uthecar. 'For that is just what Pelis the False would be about! He knows we shall search, and far. Where better to hide than where he was last seen? There are places close on Saddlebole beyond the iron gates; quickly!'

They sped through the woods, past the Holywell, past the spot where Colin and the dwarf had vanished, past the iron gates, to a hollow above a dark slope of beeches. Here there were many recesses, and caves, and cramped tunnels into the rock. Atlendor drew his sword, and approached one of the tunnels. It was so blocked at the entrance that even he would have to worm his way in.

'Nay,' said Uthecar, 'you have not the eyes for it! If he is there, cold death is your destiny.'

'But I have the nose for it,' said Atlendor. 'The cave that holds a dwarf is not to be mistaken.'

'To it, then,' said Uthecar.

He stood back, his eye glinting savagely, and watched the elf's hips slide into the opening.

'It goes some way into the hill,' called Atlendor, 'and there is not space to wield a sword. The air is foul, certain, but I doubt that he is here.'

Uthecar swore an oath, and turned away in rage. And as he did so, he had a glimpse of a snarling, fanged, red mouth, and eyes of green fire set in a broad head, with short ears bristling sideways from the flat top of the skull, and of white claws hooked at him, and all hurtling towards him through the air. Without thought his arms flew to protect his face, and then he was knocked spinning by a glancing blow. As he staggered to gain his balance, Uthecar saw that he was not the immediate object of the attack, for the furred shape was already half-way into the opening through which Atlandor had passed. There was not time to draw sword. Uthecar sprang forward, and just managed to get both hands to the short, bushy tail as the flanks disappeared.

It felt as though he was holding a half-released spring of irresistible power. Uthecar planted his legs on either side of the hole, and threw himself backwards. The hind feet lashed at him, but he avoided them, and by swinging from side to side he managed to keep them from winning fresh purchase in the ground. This just about made the struggle equal, but he knew that he could not hold out for long. And Atlendor's muffled, but critical, voice did not help. He was obviously unaware of what was happening.

'One-eyed Hornskin! Who blocks the hole?'

'If the rump-tail – should – break,' shouted Uthecar, 'your throat – will know that!'

Uthecar's shoulders felt as though they were being

torn from his back, and the power to grip was leaving his wrists. There had been no reply from Atlendor.

Then the body kicked under him, and went limp, and before he could prepare himself, all resistence went, and he fell backwards, pulling a dead weight on top of him.

Uthecar picked himself up, and looked at the body at his feet. It was a wild-cat, well over three feet long, and it had been stabbed through the throat. Atlendor stood by the tunnel, wiping his sword on a handful of grass.

'A palug,' said Uthecar. 'I am thinking that there is too much in these woods that has come from beyond Bannawg.'

Every time Colin stumbled, the sword jabbed in his ribs. The pace that the dwarf demanded was not easy to keep over such ground at night. Nor would the dwarf allow him to speak; an extra jab was the answer as soon as Colin opened his mouth.

They came to Stormy Point, and here the dwarf stopped, and whistled softly. A voice replied from across the rocks, and the sound of it made Colin's skin crawl; for it was cold, and deeply pitched, and hard to place, whether animal or not. Then at the edge of the trees something moved, and began to come towards Colin and the dwarf. It was a wild-cat, and behind it were others. More and more they came from the trees, until the ground was so thick with them that it seemed to be covered with a rippling coat of hair.

The cats milled round Colin and stared at him. He was surrounded by pale green stones of light. The dwarf sheathed his sword. A number of the cats grouped about Colin as an escort: they pressed close, but did not touch him. The remainder broke, and disappeared into the trees, spreading widely to kill pursuit.

From Stormy Point Colin ran until they were clear of

the wood. He had no choice: or rather, he had, but the hissing that threatened behind him, and the eyes that were turned on him, every time his pace slackened, made him choose quickly. But once they were in the fields the dwarf relaxed to a walk, and the loping jog of the wild-cats became a smooth carpet of movement.

All through the night they travelled eastwards under the waning moon. They went by Adders' Moss, past Withenlee and Harehill, to Tytherington, and then into the hills above Swanscoe, up and down across ridges that swelled like waves: by Kerridge and Lamaload, Nab End and Oldgate Nick, and down Hoo Moor above the Dale of Goyt: mile after mile of killing ground, bare of all trees and broken only by gritstone walls. And then, deep at the bottom of the moor, they came to a small, round hill on which rhododendron bushes grew thickly; and about the hill curved a track.

They followed the track into the rhododendrons; far below on their right a stream sounded. Above the track were what looked like the remains of terracing, over-grown, forgotten. Colin, whose angry fear had long been smothered by exhaustion, grew increasingly more un-easy: there was something here, in this rank garden set in the hills, that was not good.

The track divided, and the cats drove Colin to the left-hand fork. It ran level for a few yards, and then made a sharp bend, and as he rounded this, Colin stopped, in spite of the cats.

Before him, on a terraced lawn, was a house, big, ugly, heavy, built of stone. The moon shone palely on it, yet the light that came from the round-arched windows and the open door seemed to be moonlight, also.

'We are home,' said the dwarf. It was the first time that he had spoken for several hours.

The cats moved forward, and at that instant a cloud slid over the moon. 'Stay!' cried the dwarf.

But Colin had pulled up short of his own accord. For as the moon disappeared, the light inside the house faded. Now the house lay barely visible against the hill behind it, yet what was to be seen made Colin stare. It could have been a trick of the darkness, but somehow the building had lost its form, had slumped. Surely that was the sky through one of the windows: he could see a star. And then the cloud passed, and the moon shone on the house, and the windows threw light on to the grass.

The dwarf drew his sword. 'Now run,' he said, and he pushed Colin towards the house. The cats surged forward, bearing him with them through the door.

Colin found himself in an entrance hall, cold in the shadowless light. In front of him was a wide stone staircase, and from the top of the staircase a harsh voice spoke.

'Welcome. Our teeth have long rusted seeking *your* flesh!'

Colin recognised the voice. He did not have to look at the woman who was coming down the stairs to know that she was the Morrigan.

She was heavily built, her head was broad, and it squatted on her shoulders, and her mouth was wide, and as cruel as her eyes. She wore a robe so deeply blue that it was black, and it was tied with a scarlet cord. The cats made way for her, and fawned after her as she moved across the floor towards Colin.

'No. We are so far in your debt that nothing of you shall escape from the place into which you have come, save what birds will take away in their claws.'

She put out a hand to fondle one of the cats, and Colin saw that she wore a bracelet. In design it was identical with Susan's, but its colours were reversed: the characters here were a pallid silver, and the bracelet itself was black.

CHAPTER 12

The Mere

Uthecar and Atlendor sat in the wizard's cave and cleaned their wounds. 'It is not I that will be going out again this night,' said the dwarf. 'If Susan has stepped through the gates then if we found anything of her it would not be worth the finding. There is a palug in every tree! We had to kill a score to win from Saddlebole to the gates.'

Both he and the elf were gashed with deep wounds, and their clothes were in strips.

'She has the Mark: that may keep her,' said Albanac. 'I must go to look for her.'

'But *you* have not the Mark,' said Uthecar. 'If Susan has lived until now, she will have shown herself unneedful of us. If you must seek, then wait until day. Ride now, and palug teeth will meet in your neck.'

The noise of the opening rock had made Susan lose her nerve. She thought Albanac would be only seconds behind her, and with no idea of where she should look for Colin, she ran blindly, taking no notice of way or distance. Somewhere in the wood she stopped for breath. All the while, urgency had pounced on her back, and every step had seemed to be made a fraction of a second and an inch ahead of a seizing hand. Now she stopped, and the air quietened round her and lost its pursuit: she could almost hear it rustling to a halt about her. But this was not imagination: there *had* been a quick dying of movement into silence, and now Susan felt that the night was bearing down on one point, and that point was herself.

She tried to reason, but that was useless, since all reasoning could tell her was that she had no chance of finding Colin. And the concentration in the air throbbed like plucked strings. Susan stared so hard all around her that the blackness seemed to be spotted with light – pale flecks of green; and then she noticed that, instead of swimming in rainbow patterns, as such lights do when the eyes strain against darkness, these lights did not change colour, but were grouped close to the ground, motionless, *in pairs*. They were eyes. She was surrounded by a field of green, unwinking, hard eyes – every one fixed on her.

The cats closed in. Now Susan could see them as individuals: there were two or three dozen of them, and they walked stifflegged and bristling. Susan was too frightened to move, even as they approached, until one of the cats hissed, and lunged at her with its claws. Before she had time to realise that the blow would not have touched her, Susan jumped in the opposite direction, and here the cats gave way and made a green passage for her, and their intention was plain. She found that she could move freely where they wished her to go, but if she veered from that line or tried to stop, claws were unsheathed.

She knew that whatever the danger was that Cadellin had feared, these cats were part of it: there was too much intelligence in their movements for them to be ordinary cats, and that was the least strange aspect of them.

So for a while, just as had happened earlier with Colin, Susan was herded through the wood. The cats did not touch her, but they walked close, and urged her to run: and this eagerness showed Susan her weapon against them.

She had been stumbling at nearly every step in the flat and broken moonlight, but it was a particularly violent twist of her ankle that threw her sideways, right off balance. She flung out a hand to break her fall – and the cats leapt away from the hand as though from a burning coal. Susan crouched on her knees and looked at the circle of cats: it took some time for her to absorb this new fact consciously: she stretched out her wrist, and they fell back, spitting. They were afraid of the Mark. She stood up, and took the bracelet off her wrist, and gripped it so that it formed a band across her knuckles, then she stepped forward, swinging her hand in front of her in a slow arc. The cats gave way, though they snarled, and twisted their heads from side to side, and their eyes flashed hate.

Susan had no idea of where she was, but the best direction seemed to be back the way they had come. So slowly she turned about, and began to walk; and the cats let her pass, though they flanked her as closely as before. The difference was that the choice belonged to Susan.

Now it was a matter of fighting every step, because the cats did not give an inch willingly, and if Susan could have found the strength to hold out mentally against all that was concentrated on her, she would no doubt have been able to reach Fundindelve unharmed. But although the physical compulsion had gone, the malice ate into her will: and she was very frightened, and alone. The first swell of triumph had soon collapsed. Cadellin seemed much less unreasonable than she had judged him to be a short time ago.

Susan held out for perhaps half an hour, and in that time she had gained less than a mile – not long or far, but it was as much as she could stand. The strain was too great. Thrusting the Mark in front of her, she plunged forward, with no other aim beyond immediate escape from the pressure of those eyes. And, of course, she did not escape. The cats bounded after her, no longer milling round her, but streaming close, almost driving her, anywhere, it did not matter, as long as it was faster, and faster, blindly through the wood, waiting for their moment, and it came.

Susan was running so wildly that only luck kept her upright, but that could not save her when she came to the top of a rise and the ground ended under her feet. She fell little more than her own height on to a wide path, but she fell awkwardly and with the force of her running, and sprawled headlong. The Mark flew from her grip, and bowled across the sand towards the far edge of the path.

Susan scrambled after it, but she was too late. Below the path the hill fell steeply to the plain in a scree of pebbled sand and boulders, and already the bracelet was gathering speed down the slope. Susan looked over her shoulder, and did not pause. The cats were ten yards away, and there was something in them that told her that they had forgotten their original purpose, and wanted only revenge. She leapt down the scree after her bracelet, so intent upon it that she ignored the pitch of the slope : and after a few steps her weight began to run away with her. Her legs scissored into strides, each one raking longer than the last, her feet as heavy as pendulums. She tried to lean backwards, but she could not control her body at all. And the Mark of Fohla drew away from her, travelling faster than she was, and increasing its speed, dancing over the stones : and then it hit a boulder, and sprang into the air, and at the peak of the bound it stopped, and hung, spinning, but did not fall.

At first the bracelet was a clean band of silver, catching the moon, but then it began to thicken raggedly into white fire like a Catherine-wheel. The fire grew broader, and there was now no bracelet, but a disc of light with a round black centre that had been the space enclosed by the bracelet, and the disc grew until it filled all Susan's vision, and as the last rim of night disappeared it seemed that the edges of the fire came towards her and the black middle receded, though it did not diminish in size, so that instead of a disc it was now a whirling tunnel, and Susan was rushing helplessly into it.

The ground vanished from under her feet, and she ran, still out of control, but the swinging weight had gone from her legs. The tunnel spun about her, so that she felt she was running on the roof and on the walls as often as on the floor. She ran timelessly, but the black circle in front of her, which gathered the perspective to itself, and so appeared to mark the end of the tunnel, slowly began to increase in size, and the blackness was no longer even, but speckled with grey. The contrast grew with the circle, and colours started to emerge, and Susan was looking at trees, and water, and sunlight. Then the circle was bigger than the fire, and soon it was a complete picture fogged with silver at the edges, and that thinned like dawn mist, and Susan ran out of the tunnel on to grass. She stopped, breathless, and looked about her.

She realised at once where she was: she was standing on an island, thick with trees, in the middle of Redesmere, a stretch of water that lay four miles to the south of Alderley. But it was now day, and by the warmth of the air, and the glint of light on the water, the song of birds, and the green on the trees across the lake, it was summer, too.

Something nearly as strange had brought her to this island once before, and it was then that she had first put on the bracelet. Her heart lightened as she looked round for the person she knew she would find – Angharad Goldenhand, the Lady of the Lake. And there was Angharad, standing among the trees, tall, slender, dressed in long robes, her hair the colour of gold, her skin white as the snow of one night, her cheeks smooth and even and red as foxgloves: and in her hand was Susan's bracelet.

CHAPTER 13

The Bodach

Angharad smiled. 'It is time for you to know more of your place in these things,' she said, and she fastened the bracelet on Susan's wrist. 'Come with me.'

She took Susan by the hand, and they went through the trees to a clearing, and there they sat down. Susan felt the burden of loneliness slip from her as Angharad spoke, for Angharad knew all that had happened; there was no need for Susan to explain.

'Little of this is chance,' she said, 'for good or evil, and on your shoulders it may all lie.'

'Mine?' said Susan. 'But why me?'

'Firstly, all your danger rests with the Morrigan.'

'*The Morrigan?*'

'Yes: she is here, and revenge fills her heart. It will be long before she is restored to her old power, but even now she is a threat to the world, and all her will is turned against you. She has Colin at this moment, and will use him to destroy you, if she can. For the Mark of Fohla is a protection against her, though it will not always be so.'

'But why *me*? Why do *I* matter?' said Susan. 'I don't know anything about magic. Why can't you or Cadellin deal with her?'

'When you put on the Mark you put on a destiny,' said Angharad. 'That is what Cadellin feared. And at this time through you alone can we work most surely. For, you see, this is moon magic, and we wear a part of it.' She held out her wrist, and Susan saw a white bracelet there. 'Our power waxes, and wanes: mine is of the full moon, the Morrigan's is of the old. And the moon is old now, so she is strong.'

'Then how do I fit in?' said Susan.

'You are young, and your bracelet is the young moon's. Then you can be more than the Morrigan, if you have courage. I am able to put you on the road now, and help you guard against the Morrigan while the moon is old, but that is all. What do you say? Will you help?'

'Of course I will. I've no choice, really, have I?' said Susan. '*She*'ll still be after me, whatever happens, and Colin won't stand a chance.'

'That is so,' said Angharad. 'Revenge was great in her, but now, if not before, she will know that you wear the Mark. The new moon is always her fear, and at this time above all, for it will be the moon of Gomrath, when our magic was strongest in the world, and may be yet again. 'The Morrigan will try to destroy you before you take on the power. You must carry war to her now, and hold her. If you succeed, she may never be a threat to us. If you fail, she may grow beyond confining.

'Now take this.' Angharad gave Susan a leather belt. From it hung a small, curved horn, white as ivory, and the mouthpiece and the rim were of chased gold.

'She in her art will call on other power, and you will have little. So take this horn: it is the third best thing of price that was ever won, and is called Anghalac. Moriath gave it to Finn, and Finn to Camha, and Camha to me. Blow it if all else is lost, but only then. For once Anghalac sounds you may not know peace again, not in the sun's circle nor in the darkling of the world.

'Remember: only – if – all – else – is – lost —'

'I – shall —' said Susan.

The magic was ending. The island swung away from her into sleep. Angharad's last words came out of a distance, and echoed in her head: she could not stay awake: her mind sank into darkness beyond the reach of dreams. . . .

Susan listened to the water for a long time before she opened her eyes. Its sound brought her gently awake, and then she turned on to her back, and looked at the stars. She was on the bank of a river, which ran along the bottom of a valley among high and barren hills. Yet close by her was a stone gateway, and beyond it a drive led into a coomb of trees.

There was a road by the water, but Susan was drawn to the coomb. Road, valley, and sky were lifeless, but the gate was odd beyond the fact of its being there at all. She examined it closely: it was of iron, chained, and padlocked, and all were sharp with rust.

Susan climbed over the gate, and began to walk up the drive. On her left a stream went down to the river, and after a few yards rhododendron bushes closed in. The drive was straight, and had once been broad, but the rhododendrons had run wild in neglect, and the drive was now a thread of sand that picked up faintly the yellow of the lop-sided moon.

The water gurgled behind the bushes, and was the only sound, and that deepened as the pathway rose above the trench that the stream had cut through the rock; and everywhere the rhododendrons suffocated the valley. Their mass hung over Susan like a threat: she felt that all those millions of leaves, each acrid, leathery, breathing, alive, were piled into one green-celled body, that together they had an awareness that was animal. This may have been only imagination, but the effect on her was that every sense became sharpened, and she moved as delicately as a wild creature, avoiding twigs and loose stones almost unconsciously, never doubting that she was near to Colin.

Twice the path crossed the stream, and here there were stone bridges with crumbling parapets. The second of these bridges was almost half a mile up the drive from the gate, and by this time Susan had reached a fine pitch of awareness. Her eyes used every mote of light, and she could see all that was on the path, and as much of the borders as the rhododendrons allowed. The second bridge stood at a fork in the valley: in the fork was a bush-covered hill, and the stream and a tributary flowed on either side of it, becoming one at the bridge. The path continued up the left-hand arm of the valley, and standing close to the bridge, in the shadow of the rhododendrons, unmoving, was what looked like a man.

He held a spear and a small, round shield. The light caught the dome of his head, and touched his chest and shoulders, but the rest of him was in shadow: and he was so still that Susan could not be sure that he was not a piece of eccentric statuary.

Susan watched him, or it, for several minutes, and not once was there a tremor of life to help her make up her mind. There was no question of turning back: she knew that she must go on at all cost, and that the risk was too great to chance walking past the figure at the bridge.

There was no point in trying to force a way through the bushes: the only alternative was the stream, which at this spot was not far below the path. Susan moved back until she was out of sight of the bridge, and then she lowered herself down the bank and into the water.

The stream was quite shallow, but very rocky, and sometimes there were pools into which Susan fell waist-deep. She could not walk silently, but the rattle of the water over the boulders covered any noise Susan made, and she kept close against the bank, where the shadows were thick. The bridge itself was the worst part. It was low, and the air stank of slime, and Susan fell against things that moved away from her in the darkness.

Once clear of the bridge, she found that the banks grew higher and steeper, but she continued for another hundred yards or so before daring to leave the water. The bank here was nearly vertical, and consisted of wet leaf-mould and earth. Eight or nine times Susan clawed her way up to within feet of the broken terrace-work that supported the path, only to fall back in the wake of a land-slide. But at last she got her shoulders on to the path, and managed to pull herself up.

The drive was now its original width, and a few yards further on, a branch curled away to the right. Susan paused, wondering whether to continue uphill, but she decided to explore the branch at least as far as the bend.

She moved as quietly as ever, but all her wariness could not stop the gasp that came from her when she saw what was beyond the turn of the bend.

The path bordered a terraced lawn, approached by steps, and on the lawn was a mansion of stone, built in the heavy Italian style of the last century. All the windows glowed with a light that was stronger than the moon, but of the same quality, and lifeless.

Susan knew that this was what she was meant to find. This was the heart of the evil. The Morrigan was here – and so was Colin. Susan started towards the house, and then halted. No, she thought. I don't know where to look, or what to do. She'll probably have us both. I've got to let Cadellin know she's here: he'll be able to deal with her.

Above the door of the house was a square tower, and as if to confirm Susan's thoughts, a figure appeared in one of the arched windows of the tower. It was the Morrigan. She stared down at the lawn, and although Susan was in shadow she felt as if a strong light was on her, and it took all her control to stand quite still while the Morrigan looked out at the night. When she moved away from the window, Susan crept back along the drive.

The house had frightened her. Why me? she thought. Why couldn't Anghard tell Cadellin? She must have known. 'On your shoulders it may all lie,' that's what she said. Well, she might have told me more about it. *I* don't know any magic, and those that do are scared of the Morrigan, so I'd not be much use in there by myself. I've got to find Cadellin.

Susan had reached the junction of the paths. She could turn left, down the valley, or continue climbing to the right. She did not want to negotiate the bridge again, for now she was certain that whatever was guarding it was not ornamental sculpture. But then where was she? And in which direction was Alderley? She found her bearings with the help of the Plough: the uphill path ran nearly due west. Which is the right way if I'm in the Pennines, she thought, but not much good if this is Wales. But if it *is* Wales, I'm forty miles from Alderley, so it'd better be the Pennines. She set off up the hill.

The path continued as before, but not for long. The rhododendron tangle ended, and in front of Susan was an empty gateway in a stone wall, and beyond this, open ground fell gently for a distance, and then reared to a whale-backed ridge of mountain that dwarfed the world. It made Susan's knees weak and her head spin to look at it. But, beyond the ridge, she hoped, was the plain, and Alderley: and at least there were no rhododendrons.

Susan stepped through the gateway, and as she did, someone rose out of the shadow of the wall. In the open light she could see him clearly now, whether he was the same that had guarded the bridge or another guarding the wall. He was not quite as tall as Susan. His head was bald and smooth, and his ears were pointed, the eyes almond-shaped, glowing, and the nose was hooked and thin. His spear was like a leaf, and his body was covered with flat locks of hair, dense as scales.

Susan stood rooted with shock, and could not move even when the man reached out and gripped her by the arm. But the cry that broke from the wide mouth then, released her muscles. For as he touched her, the Mark had shone fire, and a white flame had streaked up her arm and cut at the hand like a whiplash. The man dropped against the wall, and did not move again.

Susan ran from the gate down to the open moor, but she was hardly at the foot of the mountain when there was a shout, and, looking round, she saw another armed man leap over the wall in pursuit.

But was he a man? There was something wrong in the way of his running. He was quick and lizard-dry over the grass: his legs raked forward in pecking strides, and the knee joint seemed to be reversed, while below the knee the leg was thin, and the feet were taloned.

Susan had a fifty-yard lead, but she was climbing while the other was still on the downward slope. She scrambled upwards, trying to keep some energy in reserve, but she was driven by the need for escape.

A spear sighed over her shoulder, and stood out of the ground. This pursuer was not going to risk closer contact. Susan thought to pluck up the spear and use it against its owner, but she could not bring herself to face him, nor to use it, nor even to touch it. So again and again she ran on, renewing her lead while the spear was retrieved, and watching for the next throw.

She came to a group of dead trees that stood gnarled on the hillside, and she lurched through them from trunk to trunk, grateful for their slight protection. But she was so spent that when she stumbled she could not get up. She twisted herself round, her back against a tree, instinctively facing the danger.

The creature was on the fringe of the trees, running with the spear held high. He wavered a moment, searching in the poorer light, then came on. And as he passed the first tree, part of the crooked bole seemed to detach itself and rise up before him, and there was a long gleam of light that shortened and disappeared under his ribs. He screamed, and fell.

'So it is bodachs we have now!' said a disgusted voice. 'Is there no end to the garbage of Bannawg?'

CHAPTER 14

The Wild Hunt

Uthecar turned to Susan. 'Before this night, Cadellin thought you dead; I am doubting if you would prove him wrong.'

'Uthecar!' cried Susan. 'How have you got here?'

'Is it not enough that I am here?' said the dwarf. He pulled Susan to her feet. 'For the bodach loves steep ground more than a hare of the mountain. The iron-death would have been yours by now – and that may be yet: a bodach dead, and not quietly. It would have been wiser to take his head, but your bodach is swift in thrusting the spear, and it is a long sweep that must open his throat, for it is hard as a bull's hide.'

Uthecar and Susan began to climb the hill together. They walked, since Uthecar knew that there was nearly a thousand feet of moor above them, and if they were going to be followed, running would not save them.

They could not see the house from the moor, and as they climbed, the valley of rhododendrons shrank to a dark line, and then fell below the curve of the hill.

Uthecar made Susan tell him what she had seen before he would give any explanation of his presence among the dead trees.

'But how did *you* find out where the Morrigan is?' said Susan. 'You've been very quick.'

'Not as quick as you are thinking,' said Uthecar. 'It was last night that Colin was taken.'

'But it can't have been!' said Susan. 'Everything's happened so fast! It was only about four or five hours ago!'

'It was not,' said Uthecar. 'You have been under enchantment on the island of Angharad Goldenhand. Earth-time is not there: years could have passed: it is the magic of the Lady that made it but a day and a night.

'As for me, that is simple. After moonrise Pelis the False came to Fundindelve, and spoke before the gates, saying that if you were not ready to go with him tomorrow, and your bracelet in his care, he would send Colin back to us, a little at a time.

'At first I thought to spill his pride in dark waves upon the ground, but that will come: first let us hurt his advantage. So Albanac kept him in talk, and I went out by the Holywell, and when he left I followed him here. But that valley is thick with dread, and much of it will not be answered with the sword. So we shall bring Cadellin, and while he traffics with the Morrigan I shall test the nature of Pelis the False, though I tread through a sea of bodachs to his heart.'

They were high on the mountain: the world was empty. Susan and Uthecar moved over the heather, specks in the tarnished light.

'What are these – bodachs?' said Susan.

'The sweepings of Bannawg,' said Uthecar. 'They are kin to goblins, but they have more heart – I will not say courage. The scream of blades is their only love, and if they are thick about the Morrigan we shall not win Colin easily. Will you be climbing faster?'

An edge came into his voice at this question.

'Why? What's wrong?' said Susan.

'Look behind you,' said the dwarf.

But Susan saw nothing except the hill's back, and the opposite moorland across the Dale of Goyt, like the belly of a weir, monstrously still.

'No. Where?'

'There, and there, and there, and there, in the heather.'

She saw them – tongues of movement darting over the ground, backwards and forwards, in and out, lower down the hill, green-eyed.

'Scouts,' said Uthecar. 'It is not the palug-cat we have to fear, but the bodach that follows. I would be putting a deal of wind between us and them.'

Susan and Uthecar increased their pace, not yet running, and the cats poured after them openly, now that they had been seen, and they began to call to each other in relays down the mountain with voices that were like an ache and a desolation of the soul.

Their numbers frightened Uthecar. He had not reckoned on so many. They would swamp him in a minute, and might even smother the bracelet long enough for Susan to be killed – if that was the purpose.

But the palugs did not attack, and Susan and Uthecar came to the top of the ridge. A stone wall ran along its spine, which sloped gently upwards to their left, and fell on their right to a saddle, rising to a peak beyond. In front was a valley, and more hills, but on the other side of these was the plain. They were nine miles from Alderley.

They climbed over the wall, and were about to start down to the valley, when they saw a line of bodachs cross the bottom of the saddle into the valley to cut them off. The only way now was uphill to the left. They kept by the wall, where the ground was smoother with sheep tracks, and the palugs drove them on, those beyond the wall moving a little ahead.

The slope was too gentle for Susan and Uthecar not to run, but every stride was weighted. So they staggered into the trap. For they were soon on the top of the hill, and the relief at the level ground was cut short by the cliff that dropped under them. And as they turned back they saw that the palugs that had been running ahead were over the wall, and had made a half-circle with those that followed. The cliff was not an impossible height, but the ground at its foot was only a little less steep, and it was thick with boulders. Far below a road wound through the hills.

'Do not think to jump,' said Uthecar. 'You would smash your bones. Here at least neither palug nor bodach will be on our necks. Though I fear it will help us little : see.'

Twenty or more bodachs were now in sight; and a group of three were at the top, almost a quarter of a mile ahead of the others. They stopped at the edge of the half-circle of palugs and leant on their spears, gloating, and deciding which should have the pleasure of the kill, since there was little to fear in a girl, and a one-eyed dwarf armed with a sword.

'Behind me, and crouch low,' whispered Uthecar. 'I have a thought for these three. If it should fail, then jump quickly, and trust in the Lady.'

'I've got this horn,' said Susan. 'Shall I blow it?'

'It was meant for worst than this, I fear,' said Uthecar.

But before he could say more, one of the bodachs came through the palugs' ranks in two thudding strides, his shield high, and spear poised. And as he landed between Uthecar and the palugs, Uthecar threw his sword in an underhand arc. It caught the bodach in the stomach, and sent him writhing to the ground. With the impetus of his throw, Uthecar went after the sword, and he reached the bodach before he hit the turf. In the same movement he tore the shield from the bodach's arm, and went down on one knee behind it as the spears of the other two bodachs slashed towards him. They bit through the shield, and stood out on the other side, but they did no harm. Uthecar grabbed his sword and the spear of the dying bodach, and flung himself backwards to the cliff before the palugs had time to gather themselves to spring. Then it was too late for their courage. Each palug saw its own death in that sword, and their minds were not quick enough to catch the dwarf's strategy.

Uthecar pushed the bristling shield and the spear into Susan's arms, and sprang back through the cats on the rebound. He was over them, untouched, in four strides, and on top of the defenceless bodachs. The sword flashed twice, and Uthecar was among the cats with two shields on his arm. But the cats were more ready for him this time. He seemed to be wading through black glue that draped him to the waist: bodies rattled against the shields about his head, and his sword was a spark of lightning round his feet. But he plodded clear, and joined Susan at the cliff's edge.

When the main force of the bodachs reached the top of the hill, they found a girl and a dwarf, armed, and standing on a projecting tongue of rock, so that they could be attacked only from the front, and singly.

It was no fight. For a while the bodachs strutted about the hill-top, trying to find a point of vantage, then, frustrated, they began to throw their spears, but when they saw that these were more likely to be used later against themselves, or lost over the cliff, than to hit a mark, they tried to rush the dwarf. However, five quick deaths halted them, and they stood back, shaking their heads in rage.

The palugs were unhelpful. Their way was to hunt as a pack: individual contests were not looked for, and there were several skirmishes involving blood when an attempt was made to drive them against Uthecar's sword.

So, after the first minutes, a stalemate appeared to have been reached.

'If we could last till dawn, we should win clear,' Uthecar said. 'Since neither the bodach nor the palug loves the sun. But what word has reached the Morrigan by now? If she should come, well then, good night indeed.'

Uthecar had seen palugs head back towards the Dale of Goyt: he knew what that meant. And all the time both cats and goblins were coming out of the valley, and were thick on the hill-top.

'We shall not see the sun rise if we stay here,' he said. 'Yet what else is there for us?'

'Do you know where we are?' said Susan. 'There's a road below us.'

'Ay, that much I can tell. This is Shining Tor. Between your feet the Mothan grew, and here the Hunter slept.'

'What? Here? Do you mean *here*?' She was so surprised that she took her eyes off the bodachs, and looked round at the jagged tor, her thought full of the light that had stared at her in the dying flames of the Beacon. And then a pain, cold as a razor, struck across her arm deep into the bone. '*Oh! I've been hit!*' Susan grabbed at her wrist; yet when she looked there was neither blood nor wound, but the Mark of Fohla shone with white fire, and the black characters engraved on it appeared to hover above the face of the metal, and now she could see the word of power.

'Uthecar! I can read what's on my bracelet!'

'Speak it, then!'

He had stepped across to cover Susan when she dropped her spear, and his eye could not leave the bodachs, who were edging closer, waiting for the first chance.

'It says "TROMADOR".'

The hill shook at the word. The air pulsed as at a note below the range of hearing, and the web of heaven trembled, making the stars dance, and their glittering echoed, 'tromador, tromador', down the night, and out of the sound came a wind.

It was a wind that was never imagined: it leapt on Susan's back, and crushed her to the rock: her fingers grew into every crack, and she pressed her body so close

that the rock spun. For it was a wind that would take
hair from a horse, and moorgrass from the ground: it
would take heather from the hill, and willow from the
root: it would take the limpet from the crag, and the
eagle from its young: and it came over the gritstone
peaks, howling and raging, in blazing sparks of fire.

The bodachs and palugs were rolled in a heap against
the wall, and held there by the wind. The grass moved
like a scalp on the hill.

Then as it came, the wind died. Susan and Uthecar
lifted their faces, and groped for their spears: the shields
had gone faster than leaves in autumn. But they never
touched their weapons, for twelve horsemen were close
to where they lay. They sat as still as death, and in front
of them was a man with seven-branched antlers sweep-
ing from his head, cruel against the sky.

The foremost rider was red, and carried a spear. He
lifted it, and his voice cut like a blade.

> There is a cry in the valley;
> Is it not He that pierces?
> There is a cry on the mountain;
> Is it not He that is wounding?
> There is a cry in the woodland;
> Is it not He that conquers?
> A cry of a journey over the plain!
> A cry in every wandering vale!

The three red riders, the Horsemen of Donn, levelled
their spears; the white cloaks of the sons of Argatron
parted, and three curled whips were seen; dark Fiorn,
north-king, mound-king, poised his iron flail behind his
shoulder, and the seven chains rang together, softly,
baleful; Fallowman son of Melimbor drew his black
sword; it hissed in its sheath like an adder; the sword of
Bagda was drawn; the sons of Ormar couched their

javelins behind their silver shields, and the hoofs of their horses were brazen moons.

Garanhir, the Hunter, tossed his head; his voice belled, wild as a stag.

'Ride, Einheriar of the Herlathing!'

'We ride! We ride!'

The palugs had started to slink backwards, ears flat, eyes narrow with fear, when the horseman spoke, but when the voice of Garanhir blared over them they were driven mad, as though the note of his voice had spoken to them and loosed their reason. They bounded over the heather, fleeing. But the bodachs scrambled from the pile the wind had made of them, and knelt closely together behind their shields, holding their spear butts to the ground, the blades pointing for the horses' chests. Yet javelin and flail, whip, sword, and spear were among them before they could strike, as the Einheriar swept them like a wave, rolling their heads as shingle.

Garanhir strode through the bodachs' ranks: he took them by the necks, and drove their heads together.

'Ride, Einheriar of the Herlathing!'

'We ride! We ride!'

The broken ranks scattered, and the Herlathing charged across the hill, cutting, flaying, harrying the goblins and cats back to the valley.

Susan stood in wonder, appalled at the vigour of bloodshed that the riders showed: Garanhir was dark to the waist, and strips hung from his antlers. But Uthecar pulled her off the rock, and started towards the end of the cliff.

'Let us not stay,' he said. 'The Wild Hunt has saved us – will you now await the Morrigan?'

'But look,' said Susan. 'They're *enjoying* what they're doing.'

'Enjoy? You have called the Wild Hunt, Susan. This is no toy-magic! Be thankful that *your* head is not rolling in the dale.'

They worked clear of the rocks, and down to the road, but Uthecar would not take it. He made a direct line for Alderley, avoiding open ground as much as possible, and he kept the pace unbroken through the night. The noise of slaughter soon died.

When day came, Uthecar and Susan were in a field at the top of the Edge, on the border of a tongue of the woodland. The moon was low in the sky. Susan was breathless, very tired, but Uthecar looked more relaxed than he had been all night.

'We are there,' he said. 'Close in the wood, by the Goldenstone, an old elf-road goes to Fundindelve. It will be some shield to us, for even the Morrigan cannot walk an elf-road without pain, and lesser troubles cannot walk it at all.'

'Come on, then,' said Susan. 'Let's run.'

She was suddenly apprehensive : a shadow passed over her mind from the east. But before they could take another stride, they heard a voice call behind them.

'*Imorad! Imorad! Surater!*'

And at the voice, it was as though ice locked their muscles. Uthecar cried out, and after that stood still, but Susan, though there seemed to be crystals in every joint, could force her limbs to move. She turned her head, and saw the Morrigan on the fringe of some trees across the field. She held a long sword, and her right hand was stretched towards Susan and Uthecar, the fist clenched, and the little finger and forefinger extended.

'Must – run,' whispered Susan.

She was able to walk, but each stride was a heavy wade; her body was dead as lead; it was like trying to run in a nightmare. But all that Uthecar could move was his eye.

'Try – run,' said Susan.

Her throat was numb with cold. She pushed her hand

out to the dwarf, and closed her fingers jerkily on his wrist to pull him along. But the moment she touched him, Uthecar felt the life flicker in his bones, and by turning all his heart to the effort, he could swing his legs, hips pushed forward, arms circling wide of the body, as though in water. So together Susan and Uthecar moved into the wood, which here was only a few yards deep, and the Morrigan came after them, her sword ready.

'Road – road – there,' said Uthecar. He put his head to the left, and Susan saw a track, bordered with earth walls, running straight along the other side of the wood. They willed themselves on, for the Morrigan was so close that they could hear her breathing, and tumbled over the bank on to the elf-road, and the deadness fell from them.

'Loose my arm, and give me your hand,' said Uthecar. 'The power against her is in you, but I would have my sword free. She will not be held long.'

They ran along the track, the Morrigan keeping pace with them on the other side of the bank. For all her bulk, she could move quickly. But they noticed that she was looking at the sky, and seemed to be anxious. They were close to the Goldenstone when she faltered, and stopped.

'Stay,' said Uthecar. 'She is not at ease: beware!'

The Morrigan stood, panting, twenty yards away.

'The wish of my heart to you, dwarf!' she screamed.

Uthecar threw himself to the ground, dragging Susan with him, and shouted at the top of his voice:

'The wish of your heart, carlin, be on yonder grey stone!'

There was a swirl in the air over Susan's head like the beat of a bird's wing, and the Goldenstone rent from top to base. Flying chips of rock stung Susan's skin, and when she looked again the Morrigan was not there.

CHAPTER 15

Errwood

'If I had found them before they drank at the well,' said Cadellin, 'they could have been forced to the mounds. But the water has confirmed them here, and this will last for seven nights, and in that time who can tell what they will not do?'

'I would be taking less care for the Herlathing than for the Morrigan,' said Uthecar. 'For the one I was glad to see, and the other can never be too far from my life. Ask the Goldenstone if I speak true!'

'I can't understand that,' said Susan. 'She was right on top of us, and then she looked at the sky, broke the Goldenstone, and disappeared.'

'Where was the moon?' said Cadellin.

'I didn't notice.'

'It was about to set,' said Uthecar. 'Think you she was fearful of that?'

'It may be,' said Cadellin. 'Her power lies there. But she is not helpless when the moon is down. What special charge was on her that she could not stay?'

'Look,' said Susan. 'If she was going back to the house, Albanac could follow her on his horse – she can't be half-way there yet – and we might see what's wrong.'

'Shape-shifting will take her, if she has need, faster than my horse,' said Albanac. 'But I will go if Uthecar will ride with me to point the way.'

'Nay!' said Uthecar. 'Give me the head that stays hewn, or none at all! Two swords are no guard. Take Susan with you: then sword, hoof, and Mark may keep you in daylight.'

'Surely you wouldn't have gone without me?' said

Susan, looking at Cadellin.

'I think Angharad Goldenhand is wrong,' said the wizard, 'but you are so far from your own world that I should do more harm to meddle now. Go with Albanac. But I beg you to take no risk.'

Susan and Albanac went down to one of the lower caves, where Albanac's horse was stabled with the horses of the lios-alfar. Then they left Fundindelve by the iron gates and rode towards the Goldenstone. They were wary of every tree, but they saw no cats at all, and as soon as they were in the fields the horse leapt forward, and they sped towards Shining Tor. Farm-dogs barked, men stared, but Albanac had no time for caution, and the land grew empty as they climbed into the hills.

Carrion birds were fighting among the heather along the top of Shining Tor, and they rose as clouds when Susan and Albanac passed through them. The horse walked now, and Albanac was on his guard, searching both sky and moor, one hand easing his sword in its sheath.

They rode beside the wall nearly as far as the saddle of the hill, then they turned right and went down towards the valley. The day was still. Nothing moved.

They halted in the copse of dead trees, but there was no trace of the bodach, and the rhododendrons made the valley inscrutable.

'You couldn't see the house from here, anyway,' said Susan. 'It's the other side of that round hill in the mouth of the valley.'

'We must go close, then,' said Albanac. 'But I do not like what I see, even at this distance.'

When they came to the gateway, Albanac's horse flattened its ears, but went on without hesitation, treading softly.

In daylight the place was still forbidding. Bushes and decayed stonework, dank, green, and weeds on the path, the stream killing small noises so that the skin crept in fear of unheard approaches, and the valley narrowing in overhead.

Susan pointed to the left-hand fork of the drive.

'It's just round that bend,' she whispered.

Albanac nodded. They edged forward. The horse seemed to know the risk. Albanac drew his sword as they reached the corner – and Susan gave a shout that sent birds crashing through the trees in fright.

For the terrace that held the lawn was strewn across the path; where Susan had seen an ornamental pond was now a little mound of rushes; the towered, glowing house was a pile of masonry and shattered walls, bracken and nettle showing through the rubble, gaunt with window arches.

'This is long dead,' said Albanac.

'But it was a house last night!' cried Susan. 'The Morrigan was here. I *saw* her!'

'I do not doubt you,' said Albanac. 'There is witch-magic here. Come.'

He spun the horse round, and set off back along the path at a gallop. There was an urgent need to be clear of the valley: it was as though the danger had yawned at their feet and they were jumping back by instinct while their minds raced to enclose it. But when they reached the open hillside again much of the dread slipped from their backs, and Albanac slowed the horse to a canter.

'What made the house fall?' said Susan. Her voice broke.

'No, Susan: what you saw last night was the work of the Morrigan,' said Albanac. 'We must find Cadellin, for I think I see light in this, and we may have the advantage of her.'

'How?'

'Let us ask Cadellin first: he is a truer judge of these things. But I think that Colin is safer now than he was before, and that, wherever he is, the Morrigan can reach him no sooner than you or I.'

'Are you *sure*?'

'No: but let us ask Cadellin.'

He urged the horse to the hill, and it went over the flank of Shining Tor like a banner of the wind. For this was Melynlas, the foal of Caswallawn, and one of the Three High-mettled Horses of Prydein.

They were across the hill, and going down towards Thursbitch below Cat's Tor, when they saw a shepherd and his dog walking along a sheep track. The dog ran forward, barking, but a single whistle took him back to the man's heel, and Albanac turned Melynlas aside, and halted.

'There is a house in a valley beyond the hill,' he said. 'It is fallen and overgrown. Can you say what it is?'

The shepherd looked at Susan and Albanac with only a little curiosity.

'Ay,' he said. 'Yon'll be Errwood hall.'

'How long is it since anybody lived there?' said Susan.

'I couldn't tell you; but the hall was pulled down when I was a lad.'

'That is what I thought it would be,' said Albanac. 'Our thanks to you.'

'You're welcome,' said the shepherd. 'Funny time of year for a procession, isn't it? Where's it at?'

'Procession?' said Susan. 'What procession?'

'Good day to you,' said Albanac, and wheeled Melynlas round.

'Well, it isn't every week you see two folks in fancy dress up this way: I just thought there must be summat doing.'

'But I'm not —' said Susan.

'*Two?*' said Albanac, drawing rein sharply. 'Who else is it you have seen?'

'There was a woman passed me about half an hour

since, by Thursbitch yonder,' said the shepherd, 'making for Errwood. I've never seen anybody shift so fast! She was all dressed up in long skirts and that, but she was too far away to speak to.'

'Half an hour?' said Albanac. 'Can you be certain?'

'Ay, well, say twenty minutes.'

'Our thanks to you once more!' cried Albanac, and Melynlas sprang away towards Alderley, and the turf flew about their heads like swallows before rain.

'I think we have her!' Albanac shouted through the noise of their running. 'She was there not long before us, and that was too late for her, yet it was close enough for her to see us, but she did not attack – and that means she dared not. I think we have her!'

The ride back to Alderley was faster than any Susan had known, faster even than that of the Herlathing from Broad hill to the Beacon, and the night red with wendfire. Nor did they pause to stable Melynlas, but they entered Fundindelve by the Holywell, straight to the wizard's cave.

'You must act now,' said Cadellin when they had told their story. 'It seems that she is not yet strong enough of herself to attack you without preparation, unless she can draw upon the moon. All this is moon magic. She has used it to build the memory of the house into stones of hardness, and it is there, I will say, only when the old moon looks on it. If she did not gain the house before moonset, then she is barred from it until the night, and if Colin is there he is safe for a while. You must put yourselves between her and the house while there is light, and at moonrise keep her from the house until Colin is freed.'

'We shall need help, then,' said Albanac. 'Three or four cannot guard that house. I think we must talk with Atlendor.'

They all went together, in spite of Uthecar's objections to relying on the elves in any way, to the deepest cave of Fundindelve, where the lios-alfar sat grouped in their cantrefs, orderly and silent. The only noise was a spasm of coughing that would break out from time to time in different parts of the cave. Susan could not help being frightened a little by the stillness.

They came to Atlendor, alone at the far end of the cave, and they told him what they were going to do.

'Will the lios-alfar lend their aid in this?' said Albanac. 'It is for the one night, and among hills; the smoke-sickness cannot take hold in so short a time.'

Atlendor stood up. His eyes shone.

'Can it not?' he said. 'But that is no matter. The lios-alfar ride three nights from this. We have given aid to hunt the Brollachan. This moon magic concerns us not at all. And you are pledged to ride with us, though I see word-breaking in your heart.'

'My lord Atlendor,' said Albanac, 'is it to be said of the lios-alfar that they will not fight black trouble where they find it?'

'Ay. When it deals with men. Too often they are the death of my people. We ride three nights from this, Albanac, and you with us.'

He was turning away, as though the subject had been closed, when Susan's voice halted him.

'If you won't help us get Colin out of that house,' she said, 'we'll see how much moon magic doesn't concern you. What about my bracelet? Have you thought of that?'

Alarm slid across Atlendor's poise like the blink of an eyelid.

'You, too, have pledged yourself to our need,' he said coldly.

'And do you think I'm going to help you if Colin's not safe?'

'A promise not fulfilled is none at all,' said Atlendor.

'All right, then, it isn't. But what are you going to do about it?'

'You shall have fifty horse and myself to lead them, but not until the sun is down,' said Atlendor. 'If all is not settled by the third night, the fifty and Albanac shall stay, and I shall take the rest of my people beyond Bannawg.'

Albanac spoke quickly: 'That is noble, and will serve our need.'

'It is foolish, and the vote of force,' said Atlendor.

CHAPTER 16

The Howl of Ossar

Susan and Uthecar chose horses from among those of the lios-alfar, and Susan also took a sword and a shield. She had no other armour, since none of the linked mail the elves carried with them fitted her.

They led their horses up to the wizard's cave.

'Isn't there a horse for you?' said Susan.

'I shall not go with you,' said Cadellin.

'*Not go?*' cried Susan. 'But you *must*!'

'I have thought of this,' said Cadellin. 'My duty is here, guarding the Sleepers. Only I can wake them. If I were killed, I should have betrayed my trust, and only in Fundindelve can I be certain of life. And, Susan, though the Morrigan thrives, and Colin is in her power, the Sleepers wait for one whose shadow will quench the world, and I must not fail them.'

'That is true,' said Albanac. 'We were too close to the threat to see it fairly. It is better that the Morrigan triumph now than that the Sleepers never wake.'

'But what about her magic?' said Susan. 'We don't know any.'

'That is a chance you must take,' said Cadellin. 'You are not helpless there. And if you were, Susan, you should not complain. Of your own will you sought this end. I have done what is in me to keep you from it.'

'I see no good in further talk,' said Uthecar. 'There is little of the day left to us for doing what is to be done, unless we are to be a gift to the Morrigan.'

'Yes, come on,' said Susan.

It was an awkward leave-taking. Susan and Uthecar, while admitting the logic of Cadellin's words, had too much emotion in their own natures to have made such a decision themselves. As they went from Fundindelve, Albanac took Cadellin's hand, and so only he felt the wizard's grief, and saw the light that stood behind his eyes.

They rode quickly but easily.

'The sword and shield are for palugs,' said Uthecar. 'Do not be thinking to match them with a bodach's spear. That will be our work.'

'But didn't the Wild Hunt see to them?' said Susan.

'I dare not hope for that,' said Uthecar. 'Some will have escaped, but how many? Let the sun go down, and we shall know.'

It was midday when they reached Errwood. They approached less cautiously than before, and Uthecar went about and through the ruins on his horse to decide how they could best prepare for the night.

'It will not be simple to guard the house,' he said when he returned. 'These three sides are level and open, but at the back there is danger. The space between the walls and the hill is small, and the hill has been quarried sheer in parts, and bushes grow thickly. The Morrigan can be very close and we not know it. This is where we must start.'

He went to the back of the house, and began to cut the rhododendrons away from the rock face. Albanac started further along from him, and they worked towards each other, clearing the hill in a strip ten yards wide.

Susan pulled the fallen bushes into close piles along the edge of the shelf on which the house stood, between and above the two arms of the stream.

All this took four hours, and the remaining daylight was spent in hacking as much of the growth as possible on the steep banks below the shelf. The wood from here was made into one heap on the lawn.

Nothing happened at any time to make them think they were in danger. Once or twice Susan thought she heard a dog howling, far away, and Albanac seemed to hear it, too; he would stop in his work, and listen, and then go back to felling the bushes, his whole body swinging to the strokes as though he was fighting for his life.

'I would be clear of the valley until the lios-alfar come,' said Uthecar at sunset. 'Now what bodachs and palugs there may be here will creep from under their rocks and out of their holes, and we should have little time for breath. In open ground they will not be so deadly.'

'What about the Morrigan?' said Susan. 'I thought we were here to keep her out.'

'The moon will not rise yet; until then we shall see little of her,' said Uthecar. 'But let us make fire quickly now before we go. There is enough wood to burn through the night, and neither bodach nor palug seeks fire.'

From under his cloak Albanac produced flint and tinder, and eventually they managed to spark some twists of dry grass into flames, and these by nursing were transferred to twigs and leaves, and so to the bush piles themselves. There were more than a dozen of them, and when they were all ablaze twilight had come.

They mounted their horses, and galloped along the drive to the moor, where they halted, clear of sudden attack.

'How long will it be before the elves get here?' said Susan.

'Not long,' said Albanac. 'They will have left Fundindelve as soon as the light grew poor, and their horses are fleet as Melynlas when there is need.'

They crossed the stream to a flat meadowland, where the horses would have better grazing. The sky was yellow, the black clouds of night drifting in, giving a stark quietness to the valley. But this was broken with a shock that made the horses rear, as a dog howled close by.

'Where is that?' cried Albanac.

'Yonder!' said Uthecar. 'High on the hill!'

And there by the dead trees where Uthecar had killed the bodach loped the shape of a black dog. It was as big as a calf, and so indistinct against the trees, and in that light, as to appear to be made of smoke. It put back its head, and the loneliness bayed again, and then the dog slipped through the wood, and they did not see it.

Albanac sat with his head bowed, unspeaking, for a long time after the voice had died. Uthecar looked at him, but did not move, and the weight that lay on both of them was felt by Susan.

Albanac drew a deep breath. 'The Howl of Ossar,' he said. But even as he spoke they heard a drumming in the air, growing louder, and the skyline was broken with movement as though an army was rising out of the heather, and down from Shining Tor rode the lios-alfar, with naked swords in their hands, and the blades like flame.

They halted in a swirling crowd after the momentum of the hill, but they did not speak, even among themselves.

'We are come,' said Atlendor to Albanac. 'Where is the Morrigan?'

'We have not seen her, but she will be close,' said Albanac. 'We did this minute leave the house: it is ringed with fires, and the ground is clear, though on one side there is much against us. Neither bodach nor palug has been found.'

'I smell them,' said Atlendor. 'They will come. But let us go to the house, and there make ready for what we must; for I smell blood, too.'

They rode along the drive, three abreast. The horses

walked, and shields were held at the ready, since by now the last light had gone.

It was impossible for so many to approach the house in silence, but no one talked or made any noise that could be prevented. The light of the elves' swords in the damp air made a nimbus which was reflected coldly in the leather of the rhododendron leaves.

When they came to the fork in the path, Albanac held up his hand to stop the column. Something was wrong; they could all sense it. Then the elves swept forward to take the bend at a gallop. The house was in darkness. The fires they had left a few minutes ago had been snuffed out: the mounds of wood stood black around the house, and the air was bitter with a charred and acrid smell.

CHAPTER 17

The Witch-brand

The elves did not falter. They rode into line, and in a moment had put a cordon round the house, facing inwards and outwards alternately.

'Quick now!' shouted Uthecar to Albanac. 'We must have fire!'

He jumped from his horse, and snatched a handful of dead grass, but the air was so laden with moisture that the grass would not light easily, and the more they hurried, the more they fumbled, and the more the sense of danger crept over them. But when they did start a flame the wood was soon rekindled, for it was still warm.

'Wind would have fed, not killed,' said Albanac. 'And water would have smoked. This wood is dry. The Morrigan does what she is able before the moon rises.'

'And that is enough,' said Uthecar. 'We must have light, since not all here have the eyes of dwarfs, yet it leaves us no guard but our hands.'

'We gain more than we lose,' said Albanac. 'Why else has the Morrigan starved the fire? Until the moon rises she has not the means to put more than fear and fright into us, and from the shepherd's tale I would guess that shape-shifting is beyond her skill now. She sits out there, and waits for the moon.'

'Ay, and what then?' said Atlendor, who had ridden over to join them. 'We must show our strength: thus we may not be called to match it with hers. Come with me,' he said to Susan, and they rode to the middle of the lawn, where he stopped, and lifted Susan's wrist above her head.

This was the first time Susan had been conscious of her bracelet since the appearance of the Einheriar on Shining Tor, and she was puzzled to find that she could no longer read the word of power. The script which had stood out so clearly from the metal then was now as unintelligible as it had ever been.

One by one the elves came to Susan. They touched the bracelet with their arrows and with their swords, and then went back to the ring of fire. By the time the last elf had taken up his post Susan ached to the bone, but Atlendor still held her arm high, and when the circle was complete he spoke in a voice that went far beyond the light.

'Here is bale for you! Here is a plague to flesh! Come; we are ready!'

He clashed his own sword against the bracelet, and let Susan's arm fall. But as Atlendor did so, there was a gasp from one of the elves below the quarried wall, and he slid round his horse's neck to the ground, a spear between his shoulders.

'One life to save a man,' said Atlendor quietly, but before anyone could move, a voice spoke from the hill behind the ruins.

'We come. Have patience. We come.'

'That's the Morrigan!' said Susan.

'Where is she, Hornskin?' said Atlendor.

'Behind bushes,' said Uthecar. 'I cannot see her.'

'Hadn't we better get inside the walls?' said Susan. 'We're sitting targets here.'

'And where should we be but under crushing stones, if the moon rose; and we not knowing?' said Albanac. 'If we go to the front of the house we shall be safe from spears, since only on the hill above can they come close.'

The lios-alfar had all turned to face outwards. Those who, like the dead elf, had not already put on shirts of mail hurriedly unrolled their packs.

Susan, Uthecar, and Albanac crouched below the lawn near to what had been the main door of the house.

'It is good to know where she is,' said Uthecar. 'Think you if we put our swords to the bracelet it will be proof against her magic?'

'It would not kill,' said Albanac, 'but its virtue may corrupt and gall the wound a sword makes, and I think the arrows will stop her from trying to gain the house by shape-shifting.'

'If the house should come with the moon,' said Uthecar, 'Susan and I shall find Colin within. Do you keep the door here, Albanac.'

They waited through the hours to moonrise. Atlendor guarded the fires. There was no move to extinguish them – just the reverse: they seemed to burn faster than holly, and Atlendor was put to it to keep the fires high, and the pile of wood on the lawn began to dwindle. At this rate it would not last long. Atlendor stopped in the act of throwing a branch into the flames. The Morrigan had nearly won. He hurried round, raking the fires together, sacrificing every other one for the sake of the hours left to the night. But after this the Morrigan seemed content to wait. The fire was normal, no bodach sent spears.

The moon rose a long time before it was seen, and it shot high from a cloud, an ugly slip of yellow, taking the watchers by surprise. And though the light it gave was small, and could not even dim the fires, the moment it touched the ruins they shimmered as in a heat haze, and dissolved upwards to a house. The windows poured their dead lustre on the grass, making pools of white in the flames.

'Now!' cried Uthecar, and Susan and he threw themselves up the bank and put all their weight to the door. It swung easily, and they fell over the threshold, and as she stumbled, a spear passed over Susan's head and skidded along the hall. Uthecar kicked the door shut, and the wood rattled under an impact that was made of many separate blows delivered at the same time; points of bronze stood out like teeth. But the door was closed, and even while the echo was still loud, Uthecar and Susan were running up the stairs.

'He will not be near to the ground,' said Uthecar, 'and we must hurry, since he will not be unguarded, either, and the fire and our coming will be plain to any.'

They went from room to room, throwing open the doors, but all were empty. The house rang with their search.

They reached the end of a landing, and Susan was about to charge the door, when Uthecar stopped her.

'Wait! I am not liking this.'

He pointed to the upper panel of the door. A design had been painted on it in black, and there were strange characters grouped round the design.

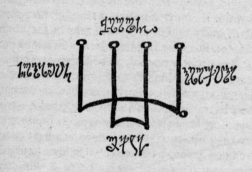

'It is a witch-brand,' said Uthecar. 'Come away.'

'No,' said Susan. 'It's the first thing we've found. I'm going to look.'

She tried the handle carefully: the door opened, and Susan stepped into an enormous room. It was as bare of furniture as any other she had seen, but on the floor a circle had been drawn, about eighteen feet across. It had a double rim, round which were more characters similar to those on the panelling, and in the circle was a lozenge, and a six-pointed star was near each of its four corners. In the centre of the lozenge stood a squat, long-necked bottle, which held a black substance that writhed as though it was boiling, though the cork was heavily sealed with wax, and two points of red light swam inside the bottle, always the same distance apart.

Susan approached the circle, and the red sparks stopped their drifting, and hung against the glass. Susan felt compelled to pick the bottle up, but as she reached the circle, the room was filled with a buzzing, like the whine of flies, and the circle rims began to smoke. She stepped back quickly, and at the same time Uthecar caught her by the shoulder and pulled her out of the room. He slammed the door.

'The Brollachan! She has penned it here!'

'That?' said Susan. 'Then we must stop her from getting in here, or she'll set it loose!'

'Small wonder it could not be found,' said Uthecar.

'Listen!' whispered Susan. 'Somebody's coming!'

There was one door they had not yet opened at the end of the landing. It was smaller than the others, and from behind it they heard footsteps drawing near.

'Back,' said Uthecar. 'Give room for swords.'

He braced his legs apart, balanced for flight or attack. The running footsteps checked, the door opened, and Uthecar gave a shout of gladness, for in the doorway was Pelis the False, sword in hand, frozen by surprise.

Uthecar sprang, but Pelis was as quick, and the sword bit into the door as it was snatched shut in Uthecar's face. He pulled it open, and ran along the short passage beyond. At the other end Pelis was disappearing up a staircase in great bounds.

'Do not follow,' shouted Uthecar to Susan. 'Guard here.'

The stairs were not long, and at the top was a single door. Pelis was fitting a key into the lock, but he did not have time to open it before Uthecar reached him.

He was no coward. Without a shield he stood, his sword in both hands, his back to the door, and there was not a stroke or a thrust that Uthecar made that was not parried and answered. But the advantage of a shield began to tell, and Uthecar worked Pelis away from the door and to the stairs, and once there, Pelis had to give ground.

Susan listened to the clash of iron, and the heavy breathing which was magnified by the stair well, and tried to believe that she could make herself use her sword.

When Uthecar and Pelis came into sight she flattened herself against the wall, and watched the glittering play of blades as they swooped, leapt, and sparked about the dwarfs with a cruel beauty that had the precision of dancing in it.

'To the room above,' Uthecar gasped as he reached the bottom step.

Susan nodded, and began to edge past the fight. Uthecar increased his attack, but even so, Pelis was able to make one vicious cut at Susan as she darted for the stairs. She threw up her shield, and the blow glanced off the rim, and dragged a long groove in the stonework of the wall, but it did not touch her, and she was through.

Susan looked at the key in the lock. Did Uthecar want her to open it? She examined the wood, but there were no marks or lettering visible, so she turned the key, and kicked open the door.

It was a cell of a room; windowless, empty of comfort as the rest of the house; and standing against the opposite wall was Colin.

CHAPTER 18

The Dolorous Blow

Pelis the False hewed at Uthecar's shield. It was riven in two places, and if he could make it useless he would have more chance of halting the slow retreat down the corridor. As a swordsman he was Uthecar's match, but his disadvantage made attack nearly impossible, and though he had got past Uthecar's guard once, the wound was slight, and he himself was losing strength through a gash on the shoulder. The girl alone would be no obstacle as far as weapons were concerned, although he was still suspicious of her bracelet, but he had to finish the dwarf quickly, or the fighting would lost its purpose.

Therefore when he saw Susan appear behind Uthecar, supporting Colin with her arm, Pelis did not hesitate, but backed towards the stairs that led down to the hall. He knew that he would not go far if he turned and ran.

He arrived at the top of the stairs, and cunningly parried Uthecar in such a way that he seemed to be weakening rapidly, and so when he faltered in his guard, Uthecar thought the moment was there, and he brought his arm down in a swing that had all his weight behind it, but Pelis threw himself sideways, rolled over the banisters, and dropped into the hall, while Uthecar pitched off balance helplessly down the stairs.

Pelis ran, not to the outer door, but to another that led off the hall. He was through, and the door closed again, before Uthecar recovered himself. Susan was the first to reach the door, and when she opened it she saw Pelis for an instant against a window that stretched from the ceiling to the floor, and through which the fires on the lawn could be plainly seen, then the dwarf hurled himself at the frame, and disappeared in a splintered cascade of glass.

'Come back,' said Uthecar from the hall. 'If the lios-alfar do not have him now his life is charmed. Let us go by the door.

'Colin, are you fit to run?'

'Yes,' said Colin. 'I'm all right. I've not had anything to eat or drink since I got here, that's all, and I was a bit dizzy to start with, but it's passed off.'

'Were you hurt?'

'No: they just stuck me in there, and left me. I suppose you know it's the Morrigan.'

'Ay, we have crossed her. But you shall hear of that later. Susan, take Colin by the hand, and when I open the door run close by the wall to Albanac. He will be some-where near. Beware of empty ground. Are you ready?' He pulled open the door, and then clutched Susan's arm. 'Wait!'

'What's the matter?' said Colin.

Uthecar did not answer, but ran across the hall to the room from which Pelis had escaped, and when the chil-dren joined him they found him standing at the broken window, looking out at the night, which was as silent and impenetrable as the caverns of a mine.

'The moon is hidden,' said Uthecar.

'But the house isn't here unless the moon's shining on it,' said Susan, 'and it still *is* here.'

'Ay, but where is "here"?' said Uthecar. 'To the valley this house is "here" when the old moon is on it, and not at other times; but to the house the valley is "there" only in the moon. So I am asking what is out "there" now, and I am not wanting to know the answer. Let us watch for the moon to come, and then through this window as fast as we may.'

While they waited, Uthecar questioned Colin, but there was not much to be told. The Morrigan had done nothing with him; he had been taken straight to the room, and locked in.

'Your time would have come,' said Uthecar. 'Susan was the chief intent, and through you they would bring her here – and so they have brought her, though not as they would wish!'

'But why didn't Pelis take me instead of Colin?' said Susan.

'He did not know how little of the power that is within you had been revealed : he could not presume to bring you by the sword.'

'Why's he doing all this?' said Colin. 'We didn't think twice about trusting him, with him being a dwarf.'

'Ho! There is reason for you!' said Uthecar. 'Why am I here if not for mischief? It is the nature of dwarfs to seek trouble, and with him it is the cause and not the cure that delights.'

But before he could say more there was a vibration in the darkness, and blurred lights appeared, which condensed into fires, and with the light came noise – hoof-beats, and the clash of weapons.

Uthecar put his shield in front of him, and jumped through the window, the children following at his back, and all three landed together on a path that was between the house and the lawn. Uthecar knelt behind his shield to take in the situation.

The elves were holding their circle against both cats and goblins. If any breached the circle they were not pursued, but were brought down with arrows, and, from the bodies on the ground, the fighting was not new.

The elves were outnumbered by at least two to one, and the cats were everywhere, a torment to the horses, and death to any elf that was unseated.

Despite her opinion of the lios-alfar, Susan had to admire their courage and skill. They were quick as hawks, yet they were calm in their speed, and they did not shout or cry. They must have eyes at the back of their heads, thought Susan.

'I do not see Albanac,' said Uthecar. 'Let us find him.'

They ran to the corner of the house, and came upon Albanac guarding the door.

'How is it?' said Uthecar.

'They attacked with the moon,' said Albanac, 'but we hold them. And you?'

'Colin is here, unhurt,' said Uthecar, 'and the Brollachan is within, so we must hold them still.'

'*The Brollachan?*'

'Ay: shut in a room of foul magic.'

'Tell me more when there is time for thought,' said Albanac. 'Just now it is labour enough to stay alive.'

But although Albanac did not overstate their danger, the fight was slackening. The palugs had little stamina, and the bodachs were realising that they had lost the impetus of the attack, and were now wasting lives. They withdrew, hoping to tempt the lios-alfar to follow them, but none went.

'This quiet will not last,' said Albanac. 'Colin, you must have weapons, and I fear they will be ready to your hand.'

He crossed the lawn, and moved about among the fires, and when he came back he brought with him a sword and a shield identical to those that Susan carried.

Colin fitted the shield on his arm, and tested the weight of the sword.

'Remember,' said Uthecar, 'these are for the palug-cat. Do not be picking quarrels with a bodach.'

'We'd be a lot better off with guns,' said Colin.

'Would you?' said Uthecar. 'That is where we part from men. Oh, you may look here, and find us at the slaughter, but we know the cost of each death, since we see the eyes of those we send to darkness, and the blood on our hands, and each killing is the first for us. I tell you, life is true then, and its worth is clear. But to kill at a distance is not to know, and that is man's destruction. You will find in the bows of the lios-alfar much to explain their nature, which was not always as now.'

The last part of Uthecar's outspokenness was mingled with a commotion that started at the bend in the drive and spread to the whole company. Instead of charging from all directions at once, the bodachs and palugs had formed up on the drive and had come in a body. They were through the circle and half-way to the house before anyone knew what was happening, but the elves were swift in their reactions, and they closed in right to the walls.

Now the fighting was desperate, since the elves could not manoeuvre, but stood their ground, using swords alone. The horses reared, and slashed with wicked aim.

Uthecar and Albanac held the doorway, the children by their side. The dwarf's instructions to fight only the palugs were impossible to carry out, for cats and goblins seethed in front of them, and it would have been fatal to have tried to discriminate.

The worst moment for Colin and Susan had come when the attack was seconds away, when they knew that they had to lift their swords and bring them down on living things. Colin remembered the games of years ago. The blade he held now was like lime, and the edge like dew. But when he saw the teeth and claws that were rising towards him and no one else, he struck instinctively, and after that the will to live was in control.

The bodachs stabbed with their spears, and leapt high to rake with their clawed feet, and the palugs added their viciousness to the struggle.

But again cold patience wore down rage, and the bodachs fell back, the elves advancing in step with the retreat, until the original circle was formed again.

Albanac kept the children by the house, and they sank

to the ground, exhausted; but Uthecar was still in the
heat of the fight, and he moved past the elves to the very
limit of the fire, throwing down his shield whenever it
grew too heavy with the weight of spears imbedded in it,
and snatching another from the mounds that littered
the grass.

He looked as though he had cooled to the point of
turning back when he gave a shout, and peered along the
drive.

'So it is still living you are, and well out of the fight!
But I see you! My sword is waking to its hilt for you!'

'Come back!' cried Albanac. 'Your reason has gone
with ghosts of the mountain if you think you will live to
take a step further!'

But Uthecar was spinning his sword about his head,
gathering himself to charge.

'Run, bodachs! Make way! For when I chance to
come upon you, as many as hailstones, and grass on a
green, and stars of heaven will be your cloven heads and
skulls, and your bones, crushed by me and scattered
throughout the ridges!'

And he shot forward past the light, into a din of cries
and the crash of blades.

'He is mad!' said Albanac. 'When his blood is less hot
he will wish himself far from this, but it will be too
late.'

The noise seemed greater than when the house was
under siege – bellowing, spitting pandemonium, out of
which no one sound emerged. Albanac mounted
Melynlas, and rode to the edge of the circle.

'Uthecar!'

'Ay!'

The voice was indistinct.

'How is it?'

'There – is breaking – of spears about the place –
where I am. I will not say – but that I may retreat!'

'I am with you!' shouted Albanac.

'Fool!' answered the dwarf.

But Albanac cantered back to the house, turned Melynlas, and broke into full gallop along the drive. A line of bodachs knelt on the fringe of the dark, but Melynlas swept down on them and, as they couched their spears in the gravel, soared high and safe over their heads into the moonlight which the fires made blind to the children and the elves. All the children knew of what followed was told by the sounds that came to them.

And then Melynlas grew out of the night, foaming, and red-hoofed. Uthecar rode behind Albanac, still cutting the air, but Albanac was low over the horse's neck, and a gold-handled sword trailed from his side.

CHAPTER 19

The Children of Danu

Melynlas halted, and Uthecar jumped to the ground and eased Albanac from the saddle. He slumped into the dwarf's arms, dragging him off his feet, but Atlendor came to his other side, and between them they half carried him to the shelter of the terrace below the lawn. Gently Uthecar drew the sword out of the wound.

Albanac opened his eyes: they were blue and clear.

'I had hoped it would not be so soon in the night,' he whispered.

'Rest you until the battle dies,' said Uthecar. 'Then you will be safe.'

'I am safe,' said Albanac. 'Here – anywhere. The Howl of Ossar: there is nothing to be done when that one calls.'

A group of elves dismounted, and made a cradle of their swords, and lifted Albanac on to it.

'We shall tend him,' said Atlendor, and they carried him to a sheltered place between two walls of the house. Colin and Susan went to follow him, but Uthecar shook his head.

'He is better with them,' he said. 'They are skilled in these things, and we shall be needed here.'

For a while he was talking, a snigger of laughter had run through the bushes outside the circle, backed by hoots and jeers, and when Uthecar showed that he had heard them, the laughter changed to taunting words.

'Was that not the foray! Well is it said that no iron is as true to its lord as is the spur! Hornskin, will you be bringing me my sword?'

The hate that broke in Uthecar at the touch of this

voice was frightening to see. He rushed out to the middle of the lawn, and drove the golden sword into the turf.

'Come now without your bodachs, Pelis son of Argad, and claim your sword!' he cried. 'I give you safe passage. But if you leave, and I yet alive, the bows of the lios-alfar shall sing to you. And if I am dead, then none shall stay your going. Here is your sword! Take it!'

There was a minute of silence. But then there were footsteps on the drive, and a black and gold figure came into the light, passing between two of the lios-alfar, who looked at him, but did not lift their weapons against him. He carried a shield, and his stride was firm across the grass.

Pelis the False took hold of the sword, and wrenched it from the ground, and he faced Uthecar without a word for him, nor did Uthecar speak, and they came together like stags. The air shivered at their meeting.

Uthecar was frenzied in attack, since the guilt for Albanac's wound ached in him, and he tried to deaden it with anger. At first he had the advantage, but he was fighting more with his heart than with his head, while Pelis countered, and wasted no strength.

And before long the passion left Uthecar, and weariness seeped into its place. His arms grew heavy, his muscles shot through with cramp, and Pelis the False continued to match him stroke for stroke. And he did not merely check Uthecar: now he was driving the blade aside, and it was Uthecar's shield that rang. He retreated across the lawn, feeling his life wane from him, and then Pelis was through his guard, and the blade sank into his shoulder above the ribs.

The pain cleansed Uthecar's mind of all weariness: he saw that if he did not use this moment there would be no other. He threw his shield from him, and leapt a twisting salmon-leap into the air, high above Pelis, and came down over his arm. The sword went through Pelis to the hilt, and the two dwarfs crashed together, the one faint-ing, the other dead.

Colin and Susan had watched from the edge of the lawn, and they ran forward and lifted Uthecar, and carried him back to the wall. Colin ripped lengths of Uthecar's tunic into bandages, while Susan cleaned the wound as best she could.

'Did I kill?' said Uthecar.

'Yes,' said Colin.

'The wonder is that I am not lying there, black in the light,' said Uthecar. 'Such rashness merits it. Are you hurt?'

'Only scratches,' said Susan.

'And Albanac?'

'I don't know.'

'See how it is with him. But go with care,' said Uthecar.

Colin and Susan went along the side of the house to-wards the corner where the elves had taken Albanac, but they had not gone far when they heard a sound that rooted their feet – the howling of a dog, very near to the house, and in front of them. The notes rose and fell in a sadness that swept the children's minds with dreams of high landscapes of rock, and red mountains standing from them, and hollows filled with water and fading light, and rain drifting as veils over the peaks, and beyond, in the empty distances, a cold gleam on the sea. And into that distance the voice faded like an echo, and Atlendor came towards the children from the shadows of the house.

'Albanac is not here,' he said.

'Not here?' said Colin. 'But he was badly hurt. Where is he?'

'He has gone to heal his wound: he will come again.'

'Why didn't he tell us?' said Susan.

'There was not time: he was called: it is always so

with the Children of Danu, since it is their destiny never to be at the end of what they undertake. They help, but may not save.'

'When will he come back?' said Colin.

'The Children of Danu are seldom long away,' said Atlendor.

'And we shall go. I have kept my word: let us ride now.'

'We can't go yet!' said Susan. 'What about the Morrigan? And the Brollachan's still in there – if she lets it out you don't know what'll happen.'

'I know that it has been a dear promise,' said Atlendor. He looked at Colin. 'One life has cost thirty: it shall not take more. We ride. Make you ready.'

Atlendor turned away, and walked back to the corner, where the elves who had carried Albanac were still huddled.

'How *can* he leave everything like this?' cried Susan. 'It's not safe, and we mustn't let the Morrigan get back into the house. Doesn't he realise?'

'But he's right,' said Colin. 'You can't ask him to lose any more for something that isn't important to him.'

'Isn't it?' said Susan.

When they reached Uthecar they found Melynlas standing guard over him. The horse pricked up its ears at the sight of the children, and thrust his muzzle into Colin's shoulder.

'How is he?' said Uthecar.

'We didn't see him,' said Colin. 'They say he's gone. And the elves are going, too.'

'He knew it was to be this night,' said Uthecar. 'It was not in us to keep him.'

'But how can he go?' said Colin. 'Why has he left his horse?'

'He has no need of it,' said Uthecar. 'You may have thought him a strange man, but Albanac was more than that: he was of the Children of Danu, who came to this land when all was green. They were the best of men.'

'Is he dead?' said Colin.

'Not as you would have it,' said Uthecar. 'Say rather that in this world he has changed his life.

'The Children of Danu are never far from us, and all their days are spent in our cause, but there is a doom on them that they shall not see their work fulfilled, since the gold of their nature might then be dulled, its power turned to selfish ends. When their leaving is close, the Hound of Conaire appears to them, as you have heard and seen. Ossar's howl shadows their lives.'

'I can't believe it,' said Colin. 'It makes everything so pointless.'

'He expected no less,' said Uthecar, 'and there was no place for sadness in him. He will come again.

'But the elves, you say? Is it that they are going, too?'

'They're running away,' said Susan.

'Then I think the better of them,' said Uthecar.

'You?' said Susan. 'What's the matter with everybody? You mustn't let the Morrigan win!'

'Can I stop her?' said Uthecar. 'Listen to me. We have Colin, and there is nothing more to do, since magic holds the Brollachan in its circle. We have killed many bodachs, and routed the palugs. When I was fighting out there I saw but a dozen in all, and when they are spent the Morrigan must needs come herself, and that is no stopping time for me. I fear her, without shame. But also, wounded as I am, the bodach is not dear to me, and for death and its fearful afflictions, and the pang of the blue blades, I will not be clamorous, either.'

'I'll stay by myself, then,' said Susan.

'You will not,' said Uthecar, and began to pick his way over the lawn to where Pelis had fallen. He came back with his sword.

The lios-alfar were backing from the circle to make a

column, the wounded in the middle, lashed to their saddles.

'How did they know they were going?' said Colin. 'I've never heard any of them speak, except Atlendor.'

'It is a part of their strangeness,' said Uthecar. 'They speak to each other through their minds, and from the looks I have seen, they hear what does not pass my lips!'

Susan reluctantly mounted. Colin rode Melynlas, who appeared to have adopted him, and with Uthecar they joined the column of the elves.

The fires were dying for want of attention; the ground was broken with bodies and splintered weapons; the house stood waiting. Susan looked round her at the scene of her failure: and that is how she saw it now. To begin with, Colin had been her only motive; she had faced impossible things for his sake; but now she felt that he had been the first step to her duty, which she was now being made to leave unfinished.

The Lios-alfar galloped away along the drive, and, but for their swords and Uthecar's dwarf-sight, they could not have kept their pace, and the spears that came at them would have taken more. As it was, three of the horses lacked riders when they reached the open ground.

CHAPTER 20

The Last Ride

The speed of the lios-alfar to Shining Tor was like a March gale, since the moon shone freely, and they were accustomed to the light. But when they were only a little way up the slope, the feeling of wrong became too much for Susan.

'Wait!' she called.

The elves halted, and their eyes were turned on her.

'We must go back. We'll not be safe this way. The Morrigan has got to be kept out of the house.'

'We are not bound,' said Atlendor. 'Come.'

'Uthecar, will you go with me?'

'My only craft is the sword,' said Uthecar, 'and that is denied me now, and I fear the Morrigan more than dishonour. Come away.'

'Colin?'

'What's the matter, Sue? You know we can't do any more.'

'All right,' said Susan, and she drove in her heels, and charged down towards Errwood.

'*Susan!*' cried Uthecar.

'She'll turn back when she sees we're not following,' said Colin.

But Susan did not even look. She came to the round hill at the top of the valley, and instead of riding along the drive, on the right-hand side of the hill, she approached the house by a narrow footpath on the left.

'She's going in!' shouted Colin, and he spurred Melynlas after her. But Melynlas would not move. The harder Colin tried, the more he ignored him. It was not the usual stubbornness of a horse: he was quiet and docile:

but he would not go.

Colin dropped from Melynlas into the heather, and started to run. Cursing, Uthecar tried to follow him, but Melynlas kicked out at the horse, and bared his teeth, so that it dared not stir, and Uthecar knew that he was too weak to trust his own legs. The lios-alfar sat still.

The path was overgrown and slippery, and the stream ran over rocks far below. Branches whipped Susan's face, but that was little to the cold that seared her wrist.

The path ended. She was at the front of the house, and there on the drive, shapeless in her robes, and surrounded by bodachs and palugs, was the Morrigan.

Susan hauled on the rein, and at the sight of her the bodachs and palugs screamed, for to them she was transformed; their hearts shook, and they fled. But the glamour of the bracelet was not on the Morrigan. She raised her hand.

Now Susan felt the true weight of her danger, when she looked into eyes that were as luminous as an owl's, and blackness swirling in their depths. The moon charged the Morrigan with such power that when she lifted her hand even the noise of the stream died, and the air was sweet with fear.

'*Vermias! Eslevor! Frangam! Beldor!*'

Something like black lightning came from the Morrigan's hand, and darted towards Susan, who threw up her arm to protect herself : and in doing so, she saw the word of power stand out above the Mark, and though it was not the word she had seen on Shining Tor, she spoke it with all her will.

'HURANDOS !'

And from the Mark sprang a lance of flame, which met the black of the Morrigan half-way to its target, and the two forces grappled each other, crackling, and writhing like snakes.

'*Salibat! Reterrem!*' cried the Morrigan.

The black rippled, grew in thickness, and slowly pushed the white back to the wrist.

Susan rose in the stirrups, and, without her looking at the bracelet, the words poured from her lips, words that she had never known or heard.

'— *per sedem Baldery et per gratiam tuam habuisti* —'

The light grew again, but the Morrigan answered her, and Susan felt herself weaken: the blackness was groping for her like a tentacle. 'It shouldn't be me. Why me?' And then the Morrigan's power reached her. Susan arched from the horse into nothingness.

When Susan opened her eyes the Morrigan was standing with her back to her, facing the house. The Morrigan had been too sure of her art, too scornful of Susan's bracelet, and what should have destroyed had only stunned. But Susan felt that she could do no more; she had tried, and failed. Her duty lay in warning Cadellin or Angharad Goldenhand. Let them deal with this.

'*Besticitium consolatio veni ad me vertat Creon, Creon, Creon, cantor laudem omnipotentis et non commentur* —' The Morrigan chanted tonelessly, her arms outstretched. '—*principiem da montem et inimicos o prostantis vobis* —' Susan crept towards the horse, which was standing as though mesmerised, and she reached it as the Morrigan's voice rose to its climax. '—*passium sincisibus. Fiat! Fiat! Fiat!*'

There was a noise of thunder in the house, and smoke began to pour from an upstairs window, then the whole front wall burst outwards, and a cloud spilled from the house, and in the cloud were two red pools.

Susan did not wait. She scrambled on to the horse, and it came to life under her, and as they sped away she heard the Morrigan cry out, then she was round the corner and on the path above the stream.

The Brollachan grew high above Errwood, strong in itself, and in the moon, and in the power of its keeper. It saw the rider in the valley, and the elves upon the hill, and it stooped to take toll of the long centuries of prison at their hands.

Susan felt the sky go black above her: she glanced up, and all she saw was night. She lifted the Mark of Fohla, but its silver was dimmed, and the words would not come. The hill disappeared; she could see nothing; the air beat with the rhythm of her blood, and the night swam into her brain; the world drifted away. And then Susan heard a voice, urgent, the voice of Angharad Goldenhand, crying, 'The horn with the wreath of gold about its rim! All else is lost!'

Susan tore at her waist with fingers that resisted her will, and put the horn to her lips.

Its note was music, like wind in the caves of ice, and out of the wind and far away came hoofs, and voices calling, 'We ride! We ride!' and the darkness melted. At her stirrup was a man with tall, proud antlers growing from his brow, and he ran with his hand upon the horse's neck; and all about her were booming cloaks, red, blue, white, and black, and flying manes. She was swept up and along with them like chaff.

And in the distance, as over a field, she saw nine women with hawk on wrist, and hounds at leash, coming to meet her, and gladness carried Susan past all thoughts but one, the memory of Celemon daughter of Cei, which the Mothan's bitterness had driven from her.

She spurred her horse faster to the welcome that sang through the night and lifted the riders from their bondage in the dark mounds, but the voice of Angharad spoke again.

'Leave her! She is but green in power! It is not yet!'

And the Hunter took his hand from Susan, and slowly drew away, no matter how she rode. It was as though she was waking from the dream of a long yearning fulfilled to the cold morning of a world too empty to bear.

More than life, she wanted to share the triumph that was all around her.

The Einheriar paled, their forms thinning to air and light, and they rose from her into the sky.

'Celemon!'

But Susan was left as dross upon the hill, and a voice came to her from the gathering outlines of the stars, 'It is not yet! It will be! But not yet!' And the fire died in Susan, and she was alone on the moor, the night wind in her face, joy and anguish in her heart.

Colin was nearly at the hill when he saw the Brollachan grow above the trees at the same moment that Susan appeared from the valley, and he watched, helpless.

The Brollachan dwarfed the hill, overtaking Susan so quickly that she looked as if she was galloping backwards. The cloud lifted, and formed a lash like the root of a whirlwind, which swung low over Susan's head, and then struck. The whole mass of the Brollachan flowed into that one point, and Colin's ears were stunned by a blast that knocked him to the ground, and a section of the hill where Susan had been slipped into the water, and the Brollachan hovered over it.

But as his head cleared, Colin heard another sound, so beautiful that he never found rest again; the sound of a horn, like the moon on snow, and another answered it from the limits of the sky; and through the Brollachan ran silver lightnings, and he heard hoofs, and voices calling, 'We ride! We ride!' and the whole cloud was silver, so that he could not look.

The hoof-beats drew near, and the earth throbbed. Colin opened his eyes. Now the cloud raced over the ground, breaking into separate glories that whisped and sharpened to skeins of starlight, and were horsemen, and at their head was majesty, crowned with antlers, like the sun.

But as they crossed the valley, one of the riders dropped behind, and Colin saw that it was Susan. She lost ground, though her speed was no less, and the light that formed her died, and in its place was a smaller, solid figure that halted, forlorn, in the white wake of the riding.

The horsemen climbed from the hillside to the air, growing vast in the sky, and to meet them came nine women, their hair like wind. And away they rode together across the night, over the waves, and beyond the isles, and the Old Magic was free for ever, and the moon was new.

Note

These remaining pages have little to do with the story, and apart from a wish to acknowledge many debts, nothing would please me more than that they should stay unread. But so many people have shown an interest in the background of the book that some kind of appendix may be justified.

Firstly, every thing and place mentioned, with the exception of Fundindelve, does exist, although I have juggled with one or two local names.

The ingredients of the story are true, or as true as I can make them. The spells are genuine (though incomplete: just in case), and the names are real, even where the characters are invented. A made-up name feels wrong, but in Celtic literature there are frequent catalogues of people who may have been the subject of lost stories, and here it is possible to find names that are authentic, yet free from other associations.

Most of the elements and entities in the book are to be seen, in one shape or another, in traditional folk-lore. All I have done is to adapt them to my own view.

For example: *The Einheriar* were the bodyguard of the gods in Scandinavian mythology; *The Herlathing* was the English form of the Wild Hunt, and *Garanhir*, 'the Stalking Person', one of the many names of its leader. (Herne, King Herla, Wild Edric, Gabriel, and even Sir Francis Drake, are others.) But the nature of the Wild Hunt seemed to be close to the Ulster Cycle of myth, so I have made the Herlathing Irish in manner and bloodiness.

That is how most of the book has been written. The

more I learn, the more I am convinced that there are no original stories. On several occasions I have 'invented' an incident, and then come across it in an obscure fragment of Hebridean lore, orally collected, and privately printed, a hundred years ago.

Originality now means the personal colouring of existing themes, and some of the richest ever expressed are in the folk-lore of Britain. But this very richness makes the finding of a way to any understanding of the imagery and incident impossible without the help of scholarship, and in this respect the following sources have been invaluable to my own grass-hopper research:

The Destruction of Da Derga's Hostel: trans. Whitley Stokes. Paris. 1902.

Popular Tales of the West Highlands: J. F. Campbell. Alexander Gardner. 1890.

Carmina Gadelica: A. Carmichael. Oliver and Boyd. 1929.

Silva Gadelica: S. H. O'Grady. Williams and Norgate. 1892.

The Black Book of Caermarthen, The Red Book of Hergest, The Book of Aneurin, and *The Book of Taliessin:* trans. W. F. Skene. Edmonston and Douglas. 1868.

The Mabinogion: trans. Gwyn Jones and Thomas Jones. Everyman's Library, No. 97. 1949.

The God of the Witches: M. Murray. Faber and Faber, 1952.

The White Goddess: Robert Graves. Faber and Faber. 3rd ed. 1952.

The Old Straight Track: A. Watkins. Methuen. 1925.

This last book, which argues that pre-historic man used a system of long-distance, straight tracks, marked by stones, cairns, and beacons, is full of the most romantic elements of archaeology and folk-lore.

The spells, and many others, are in magical manuscripts at:

> *British Museum:* Sloane 213, 3826, 3853, 2731, 3648, 3884, 3850.
> *Bodleian:* Bod. MS. Rawl. D.253; MS. Bod. e. Mus. 243; MS. Bod. Rawl. D252; Bod. MS. Ashmole 1406.

The old names have been used for the places inhabited in the story by the dwarfs and elves. *Talebolion* is Anglesey; *Sinadon*, Snowdonia; *Dinsel*, Cornwall; *Prydein*, Northern Scotland. *Minith Bannawg* I have taken to be the Grampians, although there is a possibility that it was a district that is now a suburb of Glasgow.

Fohla is the name of the wife of macCecht, one of the mythical kings of Ireland. She is an aspect of the Triple Moon Goddess.

Finally, long strings of names are poor gratitude to helpers, and meaningless to readers, so there will be none here, but I do want to thank the *Stockport Advertiser* for permission to quote the article on page 11, and Joshua Rowbotham Birtles, of Over Alderley, for being unruffled, in spite of the way I have put him into the book as Gowther Mossock, straight and undiluted.

The Weirdstone of Brisingamen

ALAN GARNER

From the first time they wandered over Alderley Edge, Colin and Susan knew that something was going to happen. Surrounded and hotly pursued by the Svarts the children fled along the track until their pursuers were halted by the imperious voice of the Wizard.

Colin and Susan's subsequent adventures through the underground mines, through woods and streams, have held countless children spellbound and breathless since this book was first published in 1960.

This is one of those books which appeals to anybody young or old with a taste for the unusual. It is exciting, breathtaking and unforgettable.

The Sword in the Stone

T. H. WHITE

Probably only the magician, Merlyn, knew that his pupil, the Wart (to rhyme with 'Art') would one day be the great King Arthur.

For six years Merlyn was the boy's tutor and the Wart learned all manner of useful things; such as what it is like to be a fish or a hawk or a badger.

Then the King, Pendragon, died without heirs. And King Pellinore arrived at the court with an extraordinary story of a sword stuck in an anvil stuck to a stone outside a church in London. Written on the sword in gold letters were the words

Whoso Pulleth Out This Sword of
This Stone and Anvil, is Rightwise
King Born of All England

The last person anybody expected to pull out the sword was the Wart but then he had had Merlyn as his tutor for the past six years.

Ghostly Experiences

CHOSEN BY SUSAN DICKINSON

The remarkable revival of interest in ghost stories at the present time is curious, for ghost stories traditionally belong to that great age of story telling: the 19th century. And yet, despite the distractions of the television screen, ghost stories are much in demand particularly among the young. Here you will find examples of ghost stories ranging from R. L. Stevenson and J. S. LeFanu in the 19th century to the most contemporary writers – Alan Garner and Joan Aiken.

Some of the stories are truly spine-chillers; some of the ghosts are gentle, some are not; but the collection should provide plenty of ghostly 'pleasure'.

'A splendid collection of supernatural adventures.'
New Statesman

'The stories in this collection have been chosen with discrimination and illustrated with a sure intuition.'
Growing Point

Charley

JOAN G. ROBINSON

'I don't want Charley. You know that . . .'

So Auntie Louie didn't want her, nor did Aunt Emm. Well, she could do without them, too.

So Charley runs away to live in a field. Her bed is a bit hard and there are earwigs in her supper, but the henhouse is familiar and comforting. She decides she is going to be all right until the sun goes down . . . Perhaps she *should* move closer to Aunt Louie's house just in case of an earthquake or a deluge . . .

Charley's week in the woods is a mixture of joy and terror, magic and misery, and from it all she gains a new understanding of herself and those she thought didn't love her.

When Marnie Was There by Joan G. Robinson is also in Lions.